White Orchid Found

Cyberworld Publishing

Cyberworld Publishing

www.cyberworldpublishing.com

This book is copyright © Olivia Stowe 2012
First published by Cyberworld Publishing in 2012
Cover design by S Bush © 2012
Cover photos: Ghost Orchid © Ggpalms | Dreamstime.com
E-book ISBN: 978-1-921879-93-7

ISBN: 978-1-921879-94-4

Cyberworld Publishing
Jindalee St
Toronto, Australia

Books by Olivia Stowe

Charlotte Diamond Mystery Series

By The Howling

Retired With Prejudice

Coast to Coast

An Inconvenient Death

What's The Point?

White Orchid Found

The Savannah Series

Chatham Square

Savannah Time

Inspirational Christmas collections

Spirit of Christmas (2010)

Christmas Seconds (2011)

Other

Fiddler's Rest

White Orchid

Found

Olivia Stowe

Chapter One: Vigil

"Should they have tried to fly in this weather?"

Charlotte turned and gave Brenda Brandon, who she knew back home in their home in Maryland as Brenda Boynton, but who she was resigned to call by her stage name during this movie production, a look of concern. She hadn't realized how wound tight the woman she loved more than anything else in the world was getting concerning this flight arrival delay. Even now Brenda's exterior demeanor was one of being cool as a cucumber despite quite evidently being deeply worried in a way the only Charlotte could discern.

"This is Florida. If they didn't fly in a bit of rain down here, there'd be little reason to have airports." The young man was being flip in his answer, something almost no one ever did with Brenda, who was one of the reigning queens of the movie box office, even though in semiretirement and by far the loveliest woman in five counties despite being in her late fifties.

Charlotte looked up sharply, because the young man wasn't usually this on edge himself. She forgave him that, though, as Clifford Boyd normally was the nicest young man. But as an assistant producer for the movie they were filming, and, in reality, the film's production manager, the logistics of getting all of the actors and film crew into Arcadia and, eventually, the Everglades rested on his shoulders. Charlotte decided he had the right to be on edge when a company plane carrying some of the stars and key production crew of the movie he was responsible for was late in arriving in a thunderstorm.

"This is hardly a 'bit of rain,'" the older, but still dashing, lead actor, David Runion, boomed out from the bank of split vinyl airport chairs he was sitting in across the cracked and grimy linoleum aisle. "And, god, I'm glad they're not attempting to land at Carlstrom Field in this." Charlotte could hear the tremor in Runion's voice too, and she knew that just as Brenda had a secret reason to be especially concerned about the plane, so did David Runion.

"Arcadia's airport isn't much better," a deep-bass voice responded. "Carlstrom may have been shut down as an active Air Force field for over sixty-five years, but this place hasn't seen much in the way of maintenance for nearly as long." Howard Holton, who had offered that pleasant observation from his seat beside Runion and across from Brenda and Charlotte Diamond, was the director of the film they were in central Florida to shoot. He and Runion and Brenda, along with the producer, Aaron Wooldridge, who was present for the film but not this afternoon at the Arcadia airport, were the nucleus of a movie production ensemble that went back almost exactly forty years. They were in Florida for a remake of sorts of the very first film they had worked on together—one that had never been completed. The movie encampment was at Carlstrom Field, south of Arcadia, which itself was on the western side of Florida, between Sarasota and Fort Myers. They were here to shoot a Vietnam War–era film, using the disused U.S. Army Air Service airfield at Carlstrom for airfield and interior scenes and the Everglades, fifty miles to the south, for the jungle scenes.

Holton's observation made all five of them scan the municipal's "frozen in the fifties" waiting room for evidence that it had improved in some way in the hour and a half they'd been waiting for the corporate jet to arrive from Miami with more of the film's actors and crew on board.

"It's OK, Brenda," Charlotte murmured in sotto voce. "Tony's fine."

Brenda gave her one of her signature brilliant smiles, but her eyes looked watery and Charlotte wasn't convinced. She took one of Brenda's small hands in hers—which always made Charlotte, the retired senior FBI investigator, feel like a whale—and, although she could feel Brenda trembling, she also felt the actress relax a bit at the reassuring touch.

The small airport's waiting lounge was dreary and drab—made more so by the gloomy, lightning bolt-laced rain beyond the dusty windows—and had all of the markings of a backwater small-town bus station. Holton had remarked as soon as they'd entered the room how perfectly 1950s down-on-your-luck drama it was and that he was glad their young script writer, Ted Jameson, hadn't come to meet the plane or he'd be itching to leave the yet-to-be-written *White Orchid Lost* movie script and move to something "farm hand" James Dean in atmosphere.

"OK, it's more than a half hour late," Clifford Boyd said, as he stood up from the bank of chairs. "I'll try to bluff my way into the tower and rustle up a radio check with the plane."

The four people facing each other in the chairs all gave a noticeable sigh of released tension at this evidence from Boyd of doing something positive, and a look of appreciation as he left the room.

Notably, the fifth person in the room, a tall, gaunt figure in a black raincoat, didn't show any relief. He remained facing away from the main group, in the shadows near the large plate-glass window overlooking the runways, and just staring intently out into the rain.

Charlotte felt that they needed to be talking about something— anything, really—to keep their minds off the plane that was late arriving and the inclement weather that Charlotte believed was seen by those present as a bad omen for the nonarrival. Six actors and film crew members were expected on the private jet coming from Miami. Those in the waiting room, coming in three SUVs to accommodate all of the passengers, luggage, and film equipment they were expecting, had driven here from the Carlstrom Field filming location to greet them. Dawn James, the young actress contracted to play the female lead in the film was the only woman aboard the jet. The men on board included Jeffery Morris, the head makeup artist—and, not so secretly, the "special friend" of David Runion, who specialized in young "special friends"; Peter Nguyen, the Vietnam-angle movie consultant; whoever was assigned to fly the company plane; and the film company's chauffeur and general heavy lifter, Sam Scarloni. But of most concern to Brenda— and therefore Charlotte as well—of those on the jet was the young lead actor, Tony Trice. Tony had appeared in all of Brenda's recent films. Brenda had, in fact, nurtured his film career—for the simple reason of motherhood. Tony Trice had been her love child, a secret that few knew.

Charlotte knew, however, and more to take Brenda's mind off Tony than for any other reason, she decided to focus a discussion on the movie they were filming. She knew movie people were best distracted by talking about themselves and their movies.

"You said the plane couldn't land at Carlstrom Field, and yet there are three planes parked there now." She addressed the question in the form of a remark to the film's director, Howard Holton.

"The Vietnam War–era F-105 fighter-bombers were trucked into the field," Holton answered. "We'll film with them and our animators will put them in the air—mostly with documentary shoot coverage—but they'll never actually leave the ground."

"I don't fully understand about the film, though, Howard . . . I haven't grasped the plotline of this remake." She was still addressing Howard, because she knew that, although the other two in the chairs would try to keep up with the conversation, Brenda would be preoccupied with worry about her son, Tony, and David Runion would be the same about his lover, Jeffery Morris. Neither, of course, could admit as much publically, which just made their frustration all the greater. The man in the black coat who was turned to the window evidently had no concerns about any of this—he had just come to drive one of the SUVs—but even though he was the one Charlotte was supposed to be most concerned about in this grouping, he wasn't.

"I'm not sure I'm clear on this movie you're making, Howard," Charlotte repeated. "Perhaps you could tell me more. As I understand, the original movie never got made."

"No it didn't," Holton answered, "and we don't have a script for the new version yet."

"The original production was back in 1972, wasn't it? Something about the Vietnam War? What part of the war?"

"It was filmed in 1972 to be 1972."

"And it was your first film together—you and Brenda and David and Aaron?"

"Yes."

"You must have been a baby, Brenda." Charlotte had turned to Brenda. The woman had gone glassy eyed, and Charlotte, who had placed a hand on the actress's arm, could feel her trembling again. Charlotte wanted to bring her back from the brink of her worry about Tony. She didn't really need most of this review. She thought she knew all she needed to know about the original, failed production of this movie. But she couldn't think of any other topic that would engage these three in conversation. As it was, David Runion looked almost like he was going catatonic. But Charlotte couldn't look after everyone here, and, it was a no brainer in choosing between Brenda and anyone else.

"I was eighteen," Brenda said in a weary voice. "I'd done some TV work as a young girl, but this was my first movie. I was to be twenty-two in the movie."

"And this is a remake of that movie? With different actors in the roles, of course." Charlotte addressed this to David Runion. But it was Howard Holton, now engaged in the topic, who answered.

"Not exactly a remake. The original movie ran into difficulties, and we've come up with a different concept for this filming. We want to do a film within a film that is couched in the original film. I know that sounds convoluted, but I think the concept is brilliant. I have high hopes for this film."

This brought Runion to life, if only momentarily. He snorted and said, "Difficulties, shit. A murder and members of the troupe just disappearing, under suspicious circumstances. And the Air Force shut us down."

For the first time since they had arrived, the man standing at the window half turned and showed interest in the conversation.

Charlotte feigned surprise, and Holton was fast to respond. "Yes, that did happen. There were cross-currents inside the group of actors and crew—not Brenda, of course. And, of course, the notoriety was phenomenal and went on for months. That's part of what we want to capture and ride on in this version of the film. The prepublicity will take us back to the sensationalized headlines and unsolved mysteries of 1972."

"Howard," Runion muttered wearily, "Just tell her what happened."

Holton gave Runion a rather sour look, but he turned to Charlotte and began to spin the tale. "One night our leading lady, Sondra Tran, and head cameraman, Scott Carr, disappeared, leaving an assistant producer, Phan Van Huy, suspected of having murdered them. We assumed it was a love triangle gone bad, nothing more. But it stopped production. The company pilot, Charlie Teng had been shot and killed as well."

Runion snorted again. "And then the FBI showed up and the Air Force got skittish and shut the production down."

"The FBI?" Charlotte asked. "For a couple of disappearances and a murder on set?"

"They suspected something deeper was going on," Holton said somewhat reluctantly. "They never said what, and if they subsequently found something, they certainly didn't tell any of the rest of us. No one beyond those three were being scrutinized—at least as far as I knew. And the Air Force was involved and had a high-ranking officer on the set, so the government's interests and sensitivities were already established. There was a war on, and we weren't doing well with it."

"Are you forgetting Peter Nguyen?" Brenda asked.

"Ah, yes. Peter was one of our actors," Holton said. "He disappeared too. But he resurfaced."

"But not until just recently, Howard," Runion said. "And now you've hired him onto the film again."

Out of the corner of her eye Charlotte saw the figure at the window perk up even more and inch closer toward them down the line of the window out onto the runways, where the sky was getting darker and the rain had, if anything, increased its intensity. She quickly returned her attention to Holton. She hadn't heard this part of the story before. Brenda hadn't told her everything.

"It's been forty years, David," Holton said. "We needed a Vietnamese consultant. Peter is an expert. We have had no indication that the government cares about him any more."

"Does the government even know he's resurfaced again?" Runion interjected with a snort.

"John Lu was your original screenwriter, wasn't he?" Charlotte asked.

"Yes, yes, he was," the director answered, his relief apparent that Charlotte had changed the subject. "He wrote the script and peddled it. Aaron and I got interested after John had enlisted the interest of the Air Force in the project. They saw it as both a good instructional film for their forces in Vietnam and a movie that would evoke patriotism in Americans at home."

"So John was instrumental in putting that film together?" Charlotte asked.

"Yes, I could say so—even more instrumental beyond that. He sold the concept to us. But he wasn't really involved in any of the . . . problems . . . on the . . ."

Holton had just wound down, and Charlotte could see that he was beginning to see a possible connection. The year before Charlotte and Brenda had been in Hollywood for Brenda to take a minor role in one of Holton's films—one in which John Lu was the screenwriter— and Charlotte, who had recently retired as a senior FBI Investigator in the bureau's Maryland office had recognized Lu as a fugitive from the East Coast, who had been uncovered as a Communist Chinese spy operating under the name of Edward Chang.

"So, perhaps the FBI interest at the time was connected with John Lu?" Charlotte said.

"Yes, I suppose so," Holton answered. "But nothing came of it at the time as far as I knew. And Aaron has never said anything about it either. At least not to me. Did either of you suspect anything at the time?" he asked, looking from David Runion to Brenda. Both just shrugged, only half paying attention. It certainly looked to Charlotte that the man at the window was paying attention, though.

"And the company pilot's murder in 1972 was never solved?" Charlotte asked.

"No, not to my knowledge." Holton responded. "They found a gun in Phan Van Huy's room—and said it had recently been fired, which was why they suspected he had something to do with Sondra and Scott's disappearance. But it wasn't the gun that killed Teng. And nothing came of that investigation as far as I know. The FBI made it all hush hush. And then when Huy died in an accident several weeks later, it seemed like the local authorities were satisfied that the murder case could be closed."

"In an accident?" Charlotte asked.

"Yes, a couple of months later," Holton said. "He was drunk and fell off a hotel balcony in Miami. By then the media seemed more concerned about the disappearances and anything else connected with the production's misfortunes than the local police ever were. As far as Sondra and Scott were concerned, they just held on to the notion that they were off honeymooning somewhere—and building a new life. They weren't able to trace a background on Scott, so I always thought they'd decided he had a past he didn't want revealed and he and Sondra just created a new life. Everyone was concentrated on the war then and how badly it was going. The couple just seemed to melt into the woodwork as soon as the media had gotten tired of the story."

"You said this wouldn't be a remake of the original exactly, Howard," Charlotte said. "What did you mean by that?"

"It was Aaron's idea really—and Peter Nguyen's after he came back to work for the studio. And David agreed." It seemed to Charlotte that, at least for this movie, Holton was trying to spread the inspiration for the film wide. "They thought it would be a highly marketable idea to make a film about the making of *White Orchid*—that was the original film. This film has the working title *White Orchid Lost.*"

"And the significance of the title?"

16

"White Orchid was the name of one of the central characters in the original movie," Holton answered Charlotte. "She was a young Vietnamese woman in the film. The movie revolved around her actions and emotions more than any of the other characters. The major dilemma in the film is hers. Sondra Tran was in that role. And it was Sondra Tran who disappeared during the original filming. We think we can revive interest in the disappearance of Sondra and Scott and give the film zing."

"Zing," Charlotte repeated, giving Holton a somewhat amused facial expression. "The Vietnamese character was pivotal to the original movie script?"

"Yes. It was late in the year of 1972. A drawdown of U.S. forces positioned in Vietnam had started and we were told that they would all be pulled out by early the next year. But we still had fighter-bomber bases there and the U.S. Army nurse corps in clinics at the bases. And the bases were crawling with Viet Cong spies posing as our Vietnamese hosts and allies. We didn't have to make any of this up to punch up the movie. This was what was actually happening there."

"Charlotte's not interested in a trailer for the movie, Howard," Brenda said wearily. "Just give her the basic plotline, dear." She stood and moved to the window at the other end of the stretch of plate glass from the man in the black raincoat and leaned her head against the glass.

"Sorry," Holton said. "Basically it was a triangle love story, with a fighter-pilot, cast originally as David here, and an Army nurse, which was Brenda's role, in one dimension, and a local Vietnamese secretary at the base, White Orchid, played by Sondra Tran, who is matched with the fighter-pilot in another dimension. There is a head nurse, who will now be played by Brenda, who tries to counsel her young nurse not to

17

get involved with a fighter-bomber pilot because they don't have a long life expectancy, and there's every reason to believe the young woman's heart will be broken. And there's a base general, now being played by David, who is the love interest for the head nurse. We'll be beefing up a love-interest angle between the head nurse and the base commander to give Brenda and David meatier parts. White Orchid is being played in this version by Dawn James—"

"Dawn James?" Charlotte interjected. "I thought DeeDee Yance had that part." Before they had come to the film set, Tony Trice and DeeDee Yance had spent time at Brenda's house in Maryland on the shores of the Choptank River, reading in on the rudiments of the script for the new movie.

"So did DeeDee," Holton said. "But we determined she wasn't quite right for the part."

What he meant, Charlotte translated for herself was that DeeDee, who had become a virtual part of the ensemble, playing the ingénue roles, and who was Tony Trice's current girlfriend, much to the chagrin of Brenda, and therefore Charlotte—and quite possibly, increasingly, Tony as well—had become too hard to work with and too much of a snot to be believable in a "sweet young thing" role.

Holton was continuing with his scenario explanation. "Dawn James is coming in this afternoon on the plane, and the young fighter-bomber pilot is being played by Troy Trice, who will also be on the plane."

Charlotte could see Brenda flinch at the window at each mention of the expected plane.

"And the plotline?" Charlotte asked Holton.

"White Orchid, whose real character name is Ngo Thi Sang, has been placed at the base by the Viet Cong, as has her brother, Ngo Van An, the role that Peter Nguyen was assigned in the original movie. In the waning months of the U.S. forces' presence in Vietnam, the Americans are heavily bombing Hanoi and strategic targets in the north. White Orchid is tasked with seducing a U.S. pilot and getting bombing mission information from him. She does that with Kyle Nicholas, the young fighter-bomber pilot, but she falls hopelessly in love with him, even though his love goes to the young nurse, named Laura Dandridge in the movie. White Orchid does get plans for a bombing mission Nicholas is going on and takes it to her home, where, unknown to her, her brother copies the plans. Having second thoughts, White Orchid tries to return the plans to the pilot's locker on the base, but is caught, and shot dead by the base general, who thinks she's just now stealing them. The head nurse has suspected White Orchid and reported her suspicions to the general, and he, in turn, is looking for White Orchid to be where she is when he finds her. The pilot flies off, and never returns, his mission having been compromised and turned into a waiting trap."

"And you say the Air Force was sponsoring this movie?" Charlotte asked.

"Yes, they saw its message as a warning to their pilots not to become entangled with local Vietnamese women and as a heroic, patriotic film for home consumption in the vein of the classic World War II movies. They had no idea at the time that they were that close to being withdrawn. We were told it would take a year or more, but we were having such a tough time there that the military managed the withdrawal within months. By early 1973, both the Air Force pilots and the nursing corps are pulled out of Vietnam permanently. We even had

19

a major Air Force strategist as a consultant and a facilitator of Air Forces support on the film, a young general by the name of Thomas Anderson. In the real world, he headed a think tank designing war strategy."

"But the Air Force pulled out and the production closed down?"

"Right. After the murder and disappearances and the FBI showed up, the Air Force got cold feet overnight, and General Anderson went back to Washington. Without the Air Force's cooperation, the production became unwieldy financially and in terms of official cooperation—and the U.S. presence in the war was winding down anyway. It was all for the best, really. We would have been putting out a film after it no longer was relevant."

"But it's relevant now?"

"Not the original film. But the mystery surrounding the filming in 1972 retains its interest potential. So, it will be a film within a film and about a film. And, Charlotte, it was actually you who gave us the idea to package it this way, although I'm not sure who got the inspiration first—Aaron, David or me."

"Me?"

"Yes, when you, a retired FBI agent showed up in Hollywood with Brenda last year, and not only solved a mystery involving the death of the costume designer Helga Lund, but also uncovered John Lu as a spy. We immediately thought of the possibility of doing a movie on the original *White Orchid* filming. We now had a handle on how to package the film—assuming we can find a good motivation for Lu's spying activities at the time."

"Helga was the costumer on the *White Orchid* film too," Brenda said in a low voice from across the room.

And Brenda's lover too, Charlotte knew. Helga had been living with Brenda in Hollywood, and early the previous year she'd been found hanging from the chandelier in Brenda's foyer. The horror of that—and the ensuing questions on their relationship and suspicions of Brenda's involvement in the death—had been what sent Brenda into semiretirement to her small home town on the banks of the Choptank River in Maryland, where she had met Charlotte, who had just retired there herself.

"So, that's why Stephen over there is playing the role of an FBI agent in your film," Charlotte gestured to Stephen Taylor, the man in the black raincoat at the window. "And why you hired me as a consultant on the film. You want me to guide Stephen in his role as an FBI agent."

Charlotte had already figured this out and had been relieved. She initially thought she was hired just to keep Brenda happy, and although she was quite pleased to be keeping Brenda happy and delighted to be able to be with her in Arcadia, the stubborn streak in her had resented the thought that she was just there for Brenda happy.

"No that's not all, Charlotte," Holton answered in a low voice. He sounded serious enough that Charlotte gave him her full attention. "The script for this movie isn't finished—in truth, it isn't even started yet. We don't have a handle for it yet. The worth of the movie isn't just in the play-within-a-play nature of it or even in the return of Brenda to the movies and the box office that ensures. We want you to help devise a plausible, movie-worthy solution for the mystery of John Lu's spy activities, Charlie Teng's murder, and the disappearance of Sondra Tran and Scott Carr so that we have a completed plot. The new movie will be about filming a new version of the movie, but, in that process, the hows, whos, and whats of the old, failed movie production being solved. We need you to help us devise plausible links between all those things that will make a great movie. It doesn't have to be what really was at stake; it just needs to make a good movie plot."

Charlotte was stunned by this. She hadn't, in her wildest imagination, thought that this was what she was expected to do in her consultant role. This wasn't just a "keep Brenda happy" role; she, in fact, was expected to be instrumental in making the movie work as a story, to help, using Holton's word, give it its blockbuster zing.

Only a small cry from Brenda snapped her out of her contemplation of this. Her eyes went to Brenda and then to where Brenda, the back of one of her hands over her mouth, was looking. All other eyes in the room were turned in that direction too.

The production manager, Clifford Boyd, was standing in the doorway. He was white as a sheet and was shaking uncontrollably.

"It's down," he croaked. "The tower said they lost contact with the plane. They say it went down in the Everglades. They didn't know anyone was down here waiting for it to come in. A search party . . ."

Brenda cried out and folded into a heap on the floor at the window, and as Charlotte lifted her bulk out of her chair and lurched toward her lover, she heard David Runion gasp and mutter a, "No, oh please no" and also collapse.

Chapter Two: Survivors and Coincidences

Both Howard Holton and Clifford Boyd showed how good they were at their jobs. They went into management mode immediately, with Boyd going off to get supplies to make them all more comfortable for the vigil to come, and Howard calling the producer, Aaron Woolridge, at the movie encampment and then organizing everything as Clifford's acquisitions started showing up, which was at the same time Woolridge arrived.

The young screenwriter, Ted Jameson, came with Woolridge and made a beeline for David Runion. He sank into the seat beside the senior actor and began talking to him in low tones. Charlotte was glad that David had someone to comfort him. It wasn't public knowledge that David was partnered with the makeup artist, Jeffery Morris, who was on the missing plane, but nearly everyone here, of course, knew. They also knew that he wouldn't want to be talking about it in the open nor that they could openly acknowledge that they knew.

While she did what she could to comfort Brenda, who was another one in the room with an unacknowledged link to one of the passengers in the plane, her love son, Tony Trice, Charlotte's FBI-trained mind was already flipping into high gear and she was totting up the undercurrents of relationships in the room.

Was the plane down by weather-related mishap or on purpose? And, if the latter, who might be involved? Who might be in the position to gain or lose by the deaths of those aboard that aircraft? And did this have any connection to the failed attempt to film a movie forty years earlier? Already the extended history of this production was taking on the hint of a curse. There had been an attempt to kidnap Brenda on the plane they took south from Maryland, and when they landed, Aaron Woolridge had said the strangest thing. After the initial sighs of relief that Brenda was safe, Aaron had remarked that at least the mishap— that's what he had called it; just a mishap—would bring good publicity to the movie filming. If that would, how much more would the loss of 10 percent of the actors and crew for the film in a plane accident be worth in terms of box office profits? And who would benefit from this?

Charlotte looked over at the actor set to play an FBI agent, Stephen Taylor, who was still standing by himself across the waiting room at the window. He, in turn, seemed to be scrutinizing her intently. Was he watching her to get pointers on how an FBI agent reacted? Wondering if she knew some deep secret that he didn't know—or maybe knowing some secret that she didn't know? She shook her head and tried to stem her racing "organizing of a criminal case" thoughts. She knew she was flipping off into the realm of speculation. Maybe the plane had come down for a soft landing and everyone was OK. Of course it would have had to be a landing hard enough to knock out the plane's communications systems.

"Stop it, Charlotte," she muttered to herself.

"What? What did you say?" Brenda asked weakly.

"Nothing, Brenda. Here, Cliff is back with pillows and blankets—and it looks like he brought enough hot coffee to drench a regiment. And there are folded-up cots, I think. Oh, what is that, Cliff?"

"A screen," the production manager answered. "It's Howard's idea. He says we should screen off the end of the room and give Brenda some privacy. I have no idea why, but he's the director."

Charlotte knew why. For some time she'd thought that Howard Holton knew the real relationship between Brenda and Tony Trice—that Tony had probably told him what it was as soon as Brenda had confirmed it to him back in Hollywood the previous year. Tony was the kind of straight arrow who, as soon as he knew Brenda had secretly been sponsoring his career, would go to the production leaders of the ensemble that had been making movies together for years—in this case Holton, as the director, and Woolridge, as the producer—and offer to leave the ensemble to avoid favoritism. And, Charlotte assumed, Holton and Woolridge were good enough businessmen to have told Tony that his talent held its own in the ensemble with or without Brenda's support.

She glanced over to Howard and signaled him a silent "thank-you." He returned a "take good care of her" in a low voice.

That's when Charlotte knew that Howard had also figured out that she and Brenda were more than good friends and housemates. Her eyes teared up. Brenda had been so insistent that no one know—about either Tony or her. She had previously voiced concern, genuine concern, about this. Charlotte didn't think Brenda cared about her own reputation with her fans but that she very much was concerned that neither Tony nor Charlotte were swamped and wounded by the publicity that Brenda's reputation would bring them if the respective nonstandard relationships were made public.

"Come on, Brenda. Over behind where Cliff is putting up that screen. There's a cot. You can rest."

Brenda didn't demure. The larger-framed former FBI agent lifted her from the airport lounge chair like she was a light pillow and guided her to behind the screen. Then she helped her get settled on the cot and sat in a folding chair beside her and held her hand.

"They must think I'm a hysterical women," Brenda murmured.

"You have a right to be hysterical," Charlotte answered. "We're all worried about them all. But you . . . and David . . . have a right to be more concerned than the rest of us."

"David? You know about David and Jeffery?"

"Yes, I'll bet everyone out there—except perhaps for Stephen Taylor, who has just shown up and never met Jeffery—know about David and Jeffery's not-so-secret pairing up."

"I don't quite understand how—"

"They are all theater people, Brenda. They can read people, and they aren't shocked by such liaisons."

"What you're telling me is that most of them know about you and me, aren't you?—and even about my real relationship to Tony."

"Yes, I'm sure they do. Our affection for each other is a little hard to hide. And they certainly knew you'd had a relationship with Helga before me. And I'm sure that Howard and Aaron—and probably David too—know about Tony. Howard revealed as much by suggesting that you be brought back here behind the screen. He knew what a strain all of this was on you. And if I know Tony, he would have told all three of them as soon as he knew for sure—that he wouldn't want to be

26

included in the ensemble simply on the strength of your sponsorship of him."

"So, I've been playing the fool," Brenda said, with a small sigh.

"Hardly that. I know you've been quiet because you didn't want to bring Tony and me into the glare of the media spotlight, but I don't really care—and I don't think Tony does either. We'd much prefer to stand by you as what we are—certainly among your friends and movie colleagues. We could just let the media find out as they will. You are easing out of the movies anyway. They may lose interest. And, I, for one, don't give a damn if they don't lose interest."

"You don't know the movie media," Brenda said, giving a hard little laugh, not in the least like her usual charming, tinkling laugh.

Charlotte could well understand Brenda's bitterness. When Brenda had been suspected of killing Helga Lund, the Hollywood media—even without opening all the way the taboo box of Brenda's sexual relationship with the legendary film costumer—had raked Brenda unmercifully over the coals.

"Screw the movie media," Charlotte said.

That brought a hint of Brenda's signature laugh out of her, even if it was followed by a grimace as Brenda's thoughts returned to what was really happening.

"So, you think I should come out from behind my fears—and this screen—and that you and I should join the others in our vigil?"

"It's entirely up to you what you are comfortable with, but I think that would be helpful, yes. I think the others here deserve to know what is at stake for you here. They are your friends and colleagues. You have the strength, Brenda. They need your strength as much as they need the opportunity to give you support in this ordeal."

27

Brenda smiled wanly, but she rose from the cot; patted her glorious white-blond hair into place, even though it would compliment her no matter how unruly it got; smoothed her skirt into flawless line; and gave Charlotte a determined look.

"I guess it's show time then," she said. "Shall we join the others?"

And just like that, the cool, in-command Brenda Brandon was back, ready to take on the role assigned to her.

The two women, the slim, delicate movie star, and the towering, zaftig retired FBI agent, rounded the corner of the screen. Brenda was about to clear her throat and say something to all assembled on the other side of the screen, but just then Aaron Woolridge appeared in the doorway to the rest of the airport facility and upstaged her. He was as trembly and pale as Cliff Boyd had been an hour earlier when he first informed them that the plane had gone down.

"A search party has reached the wreckage," he said in a shaky voice. "The plane did go down into the Everglades—at its northern edge. I'm sorry. I was told that five bodies have been found."

"Five?" David Runion repeated in a strangled voice. "So all of them."

Charlotte ran a quick tally in her mind even while she was fighting to keep a swooning Brenda from sinking to the floor. There were Tony and the actress, Dawn James; Jeffery Morris, David's lover and makeup artist; and Peter Nguyen, the former actor and now a technical consultant. And there was Sam Scarloni, the troupe's chauffeur and head grip. But there must have been a pilot too. That would be six—unless one of the others knew how to fly.

"Who was piloting the plane, Aaron?" Charlotte asked in a voice she tried to keep steady.

"We have a pilot for the plane. He . . ." But Aaron stopped there and gave Charlotte a peculiar look. None of the others were getting it, at least not until the next thing he said, and then there was an intake of breath that revolved around the room.

"Six, there should be six," he said in a confused voice. "But they said five. And that's strange too—and I had to have it repeated twice. Before they got to the plane, the search party ran on to the long-dead remains of another body. They are definite about there only being four bodies in the wreckage of the plane. But even without the body they found in the car, there should have been two more in the plane."

"Only four?" Brenda and David muttered in unison, each one seeing a spark of personal hope.

"A body in a car?" Charlotte chimed in.

"Is that all, Aaron?" Howard Holton said. "You look thunderstruck. Like there's more to tell."

"Yes. Yes, there is," Aaron said in a halting voice. "The other body they first found was only skeletal remains—it was found in an old sports convertible."

"A convertible?" Cliff Boyd spoke up. "I don't see what—"

"It was a Jaguar convertible from the seventies—a once-lavender-colored Jaguar. Half submerged at the end of a track leading into the Everglades."

Several sets of eyes turned on Howard Holton. From where Charlotte was standing, she could see Aaron, David, and even, at her side, Brenda look at Holton, whose face reflected the perfect description

29

of awestruck, and who was making a sound that could be identified as a death rattle from deep within his chest.

"A lavender Jaguar sports convertible?" Charlotte said. "I don't understand either."

"In 1972, when we were filming the original *White Orchid*," Aaron said, in a low voice, not taking his eyes from Holton, "Howard drove a brand new lavender Jaguar V-12 E-Type convertible to the set. Very proud of it, he was. He said it was the only one of its kind in Florida."

"And so?" This time it was Cliff Boyd who asked. Out of the corner of her eye, Charlotte could see Stephen Taylor drawing closer into the group than ever before that evening.

"The Jaguar disappeared the same night that Sondra Tran and our cameraman, Scott Carr, did." After clearing his throat, it was Howard Holton who made this statement in a monotone. "We all assumed that the pair ran off together in that car."

"The pair?" Charlotte said. "If there's any connection, though, shouldn't there be two skeletons in that wrecked car? None of the numbers are adding up."

Silence reigned in the room, but only for a few minutes. That pause for thought of the implications was broken by the cheery voice that those in the room initially took as from beyond the pale.

"This party looks like it needs a good cheering up," the handsome young man now standing in the doorway at Aaron Woolridge's elbow boomed out in a laughter-edged voice. It was a tinkling laugh; one quite familiar to movie goers nationwide. Charlotte couldn't understand how anyone had ever missed where he had inherited the laugh from.

"And look who I brought with me," Tony Trice continued, not yet having noticed that everyone in the room was staring at him in shock and with dropped jaws.

Charlotte was doing all she could to keep Brenda from crumpling to the floor again.

In the doorway now, beside Tony, stood DeeDee Yance, the actress who had been playing the ingénue roles in the ensemble but who had not gotten the part of White Orchid in this film. Behind her could be seen Sam Scarloni.

"DeeDee showed up in Miami to visit me," Tony continued in a chatty voice. "She wanted to visit the set but she had her car and didn't like to fly, so at Sam's suggestion, we sent the others up into the sky, and Sam drove DeeDee and me over from Miami in her car."

Only then did he realize that everyone was still looking at him like he was a ghost. "What?" he said, his voice now a bit uncertain.

"You'd best sit down," Cliff Boyd, the first one to recover, said in a flat voice. "We'd all best sit down. We have some startling news to share."

"Not Jeff? Jeff isn't with you too?" David Runion suddenly spoke out. And then he gave a gurgling noise, and Ted Jameson, the young screenwriter, was fighting to keep Runion's limp body from sliding out of the vinyl chair and onto the dirty linoleum floor.

Chapter Three: Coincidences and Deeper into the Morass

Too many coincidences, Charlotte thought. Then again, in her long career with the FBI, she had occasionally run up against the strangest of coincidences. In this case, though, the coincidences were starting to pile up.

The thought of this being a case made her groan. She and Brenda were having the toughest of times recently in trying to break away from their old lives, which, for her, involved criminal cases. They'd both retired from busy lives—Brenda from being a major box office movie actress and Charlotte from a high-powered, high-tension job as the chief investigator of the busy Maryland bureau of the FBI. Both had retreated to the small town of Hopewell on the Choptank River, where Brenda had been raised. Charlotte was also escaping from a marriage gone bad as well as her job; Brenda from the loss of a lover as well as being burnt out from living in a media fishbowl.

They had almost literally fallen into each other's arm in Hopewell on the Choptank, Charlotte surprised to realize that she was attracted to woman—and more surprised to find that Brenda was attracted to her—and both relieved to have found each other. But they had barely got themselves into being a couple when Brenda was being lured back to the movies, and it seemed that everywhere they went to try to get away from the world—either during a Rhine River cruise, in Hopewell itself, or even on the airplane en route to Florida, Charlotte had found herself embroiled in solving a series of complex cases.

It was happening here too. What both frustrated and enticed Charlotte was that she already felt the juices of the hunt rising inside her. And with each passing hour, what was happening here was deepening and becoming more complex.

The irony was that this was exactly what she had been brought into this movie as a consultant to do—to help make a fascinating mystery out of the White Orchid story.

It had seemed much simpler—although still tragic—the previous evening, after the stress-weary troupe returned to Carlstrom Field from the Arcadia airport. Once it was confirmed that the plane was down just inside the Everglades, and Tony Trice, DeeDee Yance, and Sam Scarloni had miraculously materialized, they all climbed back in the vehicles they'd driven to the airport and returned to their encampment. The airport authorities had told them it would be no sooner than noon the next day before they could learn anything about what had happened to the plane. Exhausted as they were, they still had to run the gauntlet of concerned and worried cast and crew that were gathered at Carlstrom Field upon their arrival.

"Encampment" was somewhat of a misnomer for the facilities at Carlstrom Field. The external appearance of the buildings had been designed to look like the primitive conditions of a wartime military airfield and field hospital, surrounded by defensive trenches and a series of barbed-wire fences, holding back scrub and tropical jungle. Inside the buildings, however, all stops had been taken out to provide the actors and crew a luxurious environment. There were two buildings containing suites for the principal actors and production people and single rooms with private baths for the rest, with the men in one and women in another. Between them was a sprawling building with the offices, some indoor studio space, the lounges, and the cafeteria, private dining rooms, and a small auditorium where they all met up for meals, business, and company. The domestic staff lived in another building away from the main ones.

When those who had been at the airport returned, they were met by those who had stayed behind, including the young actress playing the White Orchid role, Claire Yang; Lee Tranh Vin, playing the role of her brother, and Cameron Jacks, now in the role of Scott Carr, the cameraman who disappeared. Even though everyone was in mild shock, all of these actors were new to the troupe and weren't as vested in the tragic event of the plane crash—or even the possibility that the body of the original White Orchid and/or cameraman had also been found. So, after receiving a briefing during the communal dinner that had been laid out in the buffet room, they all dispersed to deal with the tension in their separate ways.

Even before dinner, a nearly hysterical David Runion had retreated to his suite, accompanied by a clucking Ted Jameson. Charlotte knew, looking at the faces around her, that she wasn't the only one who thought that Ted was wasting no time in an effort to step into the place of Jeffery Morris, presumed, but not yet confirmed lost in the plane crash, in David's favor—and, most likely in his bed as well. She equally had no doubt that Ted wouldn't be sleeping in his own rooms that night.

Slowly the remainder of the cast and crew drifted away from the lounge and to their own—or someone else's—beds, leaving only Brenda, Charlotte, and Tony. Brenda had declared her relationship to Tony for all who didn't know after he had miraculously appeared at the airport, and the only one who seemed noticeably shaken by the revelation had been Tony's maybe girlfriend, DeeDee Yance, who wasn't a part of this movie troupe—at least yet. Her reaction was understandably one of shock, because it hadn't been more than a couple of weeks since she had revealed her jealousy of Brenda to Tony and charged that Brenda was trying to seduce him.

DeeDee too had left the group—rather earlier than the others—visibly being upset at how Brenda and Tony were clinging to each other in the wake of the supposition that Tony had gone down in the plane crash. The young actress was equally miffed when, calling her a guest of Tony's rather than one of the ensemble, Clifford Boyd had assigned her a room and bath—not a suite—in the women's building.

"It's just us now," Charlotte said, as they waved Cliff Boyd off, who said he had to go wait in the reception room because another member of the crew was expected. "And it's been a long, trying day for us too. I think you can let go of Tony now and come to bed. He's real . . . and alive. He'll be here in the morning when we get up."

"Come to bed? When we get up?" Brenda said, pronouncing the words slowly and distinctly. "My goodness, Charlotte, is this a proposition?" Brenda's signature tinkling laugh was back.

"I certainly hope it is," Charlotte answered. "As you could see, no one—other than DeeDee—was bowled over that Tony is your son.

I'm quite sure that none of them would bat an eye at having you and I confirmed as partners either. If I move into your suite—like in ten minutes—DeeDee could stop pouting too. She could have my suite."

"Go on, Brenda—or should I call you mother now?" Tony said. "It's time I went to bed too. They are getting together a crew to go up to the crash scene tomorrow, and I'll have to go. Aaron said they might as well do some filming there. They can use the footage in the movie. He says it will fit right in."

"That seems a little ghoulish," Brenda said. "It's been forty years and I barely knew Sondra Tran, but if that's her in the car out in the Everglades, I can't help but be sad that she's been out there all these years with life just going on for the rest of us. And there are the others in the plane crash . . ."

"Yes, it does seem ghoulish, rather," Tony answered. "But it's also fortuitous, and I don't think it really disrespects any of the dead. I might be able to help with something at the crash scene, so I probably should go there anyway. And Howard's Jag—if it is Howard's Jag—that they found nearby. That also can be used in footage. Howard is already thinking of all sorts of shots from this that can be used in the opening credits film segment. We do know that the disappearance of the actress who played White Orchid originally is probably going to be the centerpiece of our new film. So, finding her body, if it's her, is fortuitous also."

"We seem to have a lot of fortuitous going around," Brenda murmured. "And coincidences."

"Some of what is fortuitous was quite nice," Charlotte said. "You coming in DeeDee's car rather than being in the airplane. But what is DeeDee doing here—other than being an unintentional lifesaver?"

"She hasn't given up on her campaign to land the young nurse's role in the film," Tony answered. "You know how stubborn DeeDee can be."

"The role has already been cast," Brenda said. "Dawn James was cast in that role."

"But Dawn James is presumed dead in the plane crash and DeeDee is here," Charlotte said. "Talk about fortuitous."

The three looked at each other with a thousand thoughts going through each of their brains but no one saying anything. Charlotte decided to find out just how close DeeDee came to that company jet in Miami.

Tony was about to speak, though, when they were interrupted by Cliff returning to the room with a handsome and trim gray-haired man with a Florida tan and smile. He was immaculately dressed in khaki trousers and a polo shirt showing off a well-developed and maintained physique.

"This is the last of ours to arrive," Cliff called out. "I've just shown him his room, but he'd seen that a few of you were still up and said he wanted to start meeting people as soon as possible. This is Ed Winslow, our military technical consultant. He's a retired Air Force colonel, flew in the Vietnam War, and is heavy decorated. Ed, Brenda Brandon, who I'm sure you recognize. She's playing the head nurse in the film. Charlotte Diamond, like you a technical adviser. She's advising on the FBI because we have an angle on that in this film. And Tony Trice, Brenda's son. He's playing the young bomber pilot in the film. You no doubt will be working closely with him."

"So, do you know anything about flying a plane, Tony?" Ed asked. It was more of a line to start conversation than a grilling, though.

"I have my flying license, yes," Tony answered, "and I know my way around small planes. But I haven't flown anything like the fighter-bombers you flew in the Vietnam War."

Cliff disappeared then, and the conversation was renewed, although in a desultory fashion. It was clear that Brenda was worn out.

This time it was Tony who suggested that they go to bed, and he said that, if Charlotte and Ed didn't mind, he'd take Brenda off for a few moments of more personal conversation.

Charlotte had been impressed that Ed hadn't done the usual jaw drop and tongue wag with Brenda in the room but, instead, had divided his attention more equally among the three, with rather more emphasis going to Charlotte concerning her FBI background. Therefore, he and Charlotte, who were deep in a discussion on what each assumed a technical adviser was to do on this film, just smiled and waved the other two away.

As Brenda left, she brushed by Charlotte and leaned down and murmured, "Did you mean it about letting DeeDee have your suite?"

"Yes, of course. I'll be up in just a few moments. Before you go to bed, perhaps you can stop at DeeDee's room and tell her she can make the switch, if she wishes. You can show her where it is and retrieve a nightgown and my toiletries and something for me to wear tomorrow. Here's a key. I still have one. I'm betting DeeDee will be entrenched in the suite before you can gather all of that together."

"I'll be happy to do that. Then I'll leave the door to our suite unlocked for you. We'll see about getting you a key for that in the morning."

"Then you and your wife live in Florida," Charlotte said as her conversation with the retired Air Force colonel resumed.

"I live up in Melbourne, on the east coast, yes. In a retirement community. I'm a widower. My wife died nearly a year ago."

"Oh, I'm sorry to hear that."

"It was a good marriage and we raised three sons, all doing very well—well enough that they have full lives of their own, thousands of miles away from me. I recommend marriage and child rearing highly."

"I wish I could say the same," Charlotte said. "I'm divorced from a rat who ran off with his secretary—but who keeps coming back regularly to irritate me and to make my life complicated. And no children either to be a comfort—or attention-getting burden—to me."

"If he left you, he must have been not just a rat, but a very dumb rat," Ed said.

Charlotte hoped he couldn't see her blush under the tan she'd been cultivating.

"You came all the way from Melbourne today—in the rain we had?"

"The rain isn't as bad on the east coast. But, no, I was visiting with friends in Miami. I came from over there by car, and I think I was driving in the tail end of the rain."

"You were staying with friends?"

"No. I was in a hotel next to the airport in Kendall, south of Miami. I won't do that again. Too much noise. I had no idea that an executive airport could be that busy."

"But you didn't meet up with those in the movie crew coming over from Miami today? They flew out of the airport, I'm told."

"No, thank god. Clifford Boyd told me about the plane crash. It was fortuitous—at least for me—that I didn't know they were coming from there the same day. Of course, I have my car and I want to have it here with me, so I wouldn't have accepted an invitation to fly. I'm lost without a car. This is America, you know. Everyone must have their wheels."

"Yes, this is America," Charlotte said. But her thoughts were locked on that "fortuitous" word. So much was happening that was a coincidence and that was fortuitous. Much too much. But Ed was smiling his winning smile and had asked her another question about working for the FBI and she was off again on an agreeable conversation.

Their moment of conversation stretched out to an hour. By the time Charlotte entered Brenda's suite, she found her lover had already drifted off to sleep. Knowing Brenda needed the rest, when she herself was ready for bed, Charlotte just slipped between the sheets and folded Brenda into her arms. With a contented sigh, Brenda molded her body to Charlotte's, and within minutes Charlotte also was asleep.

Chapter four: On the Case

"And now he's an influential conservative political commentator—operating out of northern Virginia. He says he intends to stay outside Washington's Beltway but to keep an eagle eye on what the politicians are doing there."

"Oh, he's *that* Thomas Anderson," Charlotte said. "I hadn't made the connection. I've read that he is possibly the most influential man, given his radio market-share bully pulpit, on the conservative right in the country today."

"I think even that assessment might underrate the power he has," Ed Winslow said, with a sour look on his face. "He burps and three-quarters of our representatives in Congress get indigestion. If there ever can be an institutional icon on the right, it would be Thomas Anderson. And, for my money, he gets farther out there with every passing month."

Charlotte, Ed Winslow, and Ted Jameson were sitting around a table in a small conference room and Winslow was telling them what had happened to the brigadier general who had been the official Air Force consultant for the original *White Orchid* movie. After the Vietnam

War, he'd left the Air Force, had represented the district of a rural southern state in the U.S. House of Representatives for one term, and then had moved into the world of conservative lobbies, ending up, now hitting eighty, as a demigod radio commentator on the far right.

Ted Jameson had called the late-morning meeting to get started on pulling together a script for the new version of the movie. Charlotte had slept late—for her—as she'd been weary from the stress of the previous day. She and Ed Winslow, however, were nearly the only ones who appeared for breakfast anywhere close to the breakfast hour, so the two of them just picked up their conversation from the previous night as they had the groaning buffet board nearly to themselves.

Charlotte was to learn that film companies—at least this one— didn't do mornings unless the film scenes demanded it. And, in view of the harrowing events of the previous day, the cast and crew were especially slow in rising and getting started this morning. Jameson had appeared an hour after the time he'd previously given Charlotte to start this brainstorming session. He had sauntered in all sassy and happy, though, and all smiles, so Charlotte decided his comforting session with David Runion the previous night had been a success for him. She racked it up to just another fortuitous development flowing out of the fact that David's lover, the head makeup artist, Jeffery Morris, quite likely had gone down in the Everglades with the production company's corporate jet.

Brenda hadn't managed to get up yet either. When Charlotte had begun to stir—herself having been awake for a half hour or more, mulling, as was her inspector's habit, what she knew so far of what was transpiring on this film set—Brenda just groaned and turned toward the wall. It was ghoulish to be looking at all of the possibilities of the plane having gone down, but Charlotte had an excuse for doing so. She was supposed to help make a blockbuster movie out of the original filming of *White Orchid* and to pull an engaging mystery or two out of those events of forty years previously. The coincidence of finding the car— and at least one of the people who had disappeared in the earlier period—with finding the downed plane was already starting to provide an "unbelievable, but true" plotline for this film.

Brenda had awakened enough to tell Charlotte that she couldn't possibly get up yet and to pass on her excuses to those at breakfast. Charlotte had said she would, but that had been unnecessary. With the exception of the retired Air Force pilot and, later, the screenwriter, the others weren't any more anxious to rise and shine than Brenda had been.

"I feel like I didn't sleep at all," Brenda murmured. Charlotte didn't demur, but she'd been awake enough herself to know that Brenda had been dead to the world.

"I felt like I heard planes landing and taking off all night."

"That's natural considering what happened yesterday," Charlotte answered. But it was, in fact, strange to hear Brenda say that. It had seemed to Charlotte, as well, that there had been a plane landing just outside their building. She had awakened from something like that to hear what sounded like it taking off again almost immediately. She'd written it off then as a reaction to the previous day's events, but now that she'd heard that Brenda experienced the same thing, it took on a surreal tinge.

Of course a lot of what was going on was surreal—but that didn't throw Charlotte. She'd had a full life's career of surreal happenings.

When Charlotte met with Winslow and Jameson after breakfast, Ted gave a summary on all of the principal characters in the original *White Orchid* cast and crew but stumbled on identifying Thomas Anderson. Ed Winslow, who had been just starting as a pilot when Anderson was considered a primary air-war strategist as the U.S. bombing phase of North Vietnam was wearing down, was able to tell them about Anderson.

"He's the biggest reason I jumped at the chance to be the military adviser on this movie," Winslow said. "Anderson was almost a god in those days. I don't know how the movies rated landing him as an adviser, but the Air Force must have really wanted to back the movie."

"How did the Air Force become involved in the *White Orchid* production?" Charlotte asked. "I understand that the whole concept was conceived and promoted by the screenwriter on that, John Lu."

"It's not that unusual for the screenwriter to provide the inspiration and the guts for a movie," Ted Jameson answered. Charlotte thought he was being a bit defensive.

"But to the extent that John—?"

Ted was looking past Charlotte rather than at her, and she turned to look at what he was staring at.

Clifford Boyd was standing in the doorway. And the look on his face harkened Charlotte back to the previous afternoon when he'd come to the doorway of the airport lounge in Arcadia to tell them that the company's plane had crashed.

"I'm sorry to interrupt. But the sheriffs from two counties— this one and the one where the plane went down—are gathering everyone in the lounge. I'm afraid . . . well, they said not to say anything. Please come into the main lounge."

44

The sheriffs of DeSoto County, where Carlstrom Field was located, and Collier County, where the plane had gone down, each looked the part of a rural southern county sheriff. They were both bulky, intimidating, and no-nonsense-looking lawmen in brown uniforms. And they were both giving each of the cast and crew, as they stumbled into the room in various degrees of wakefulness and dishabille, hard looks.

Aaron Woolridge was standing beside the two sheriffs on the top step of the main doorway leading into the lounge, a trembling coffee mug in one hand and looking as distressed as Clifford had looked in the doorway of the conference room just now.

"These gentlemen are the law enforcement in the two counties related to our film camp and the location of the company plane that went down yesterday," Woolridge said when it was thought that everyone in the cast and crew were present. "They are investigating the crash—and also the car and body they found, which may relate to our original filming of *White Orchid* here. I've pledged that we all will cooperate with them in any way we can. Sheriff Gordon. You wanted to say something to us before you get further into your investigation?" As the sheriff was clearing this throat, Woolridge turned to the room to further identify him. "Sheriff Gordon is the sheriff of Collier County, the . . . accident scene."

"Yes, thank you, Mr. Woolridge." Billy Ray Gordon turned toward the assembly and set his face in a serious mold. "Normally we would handle all of this down in Collier County. But the crash investigators at the scene have completed their preliminary investigation, and I'm afraid it's clear that the plane was tampered with. So, we're going to have to talk with each—"

The rest of his sentence was obliterated by the hubbub that rolled across the room.

It was Ed Winslow who spoke up. "Do you mean that you think the plane was sabotaged?"

"Yes, I'm afraid so," was Gordon's answer.

In the even greater yammering this caused around the room, Charlotte barely noticed that the other sheriff, Roy Reynolds of DeSoto County, had sidled up to her.

"Excuse me, are you Charlotte Diamond?" he asked, leaning his mouth in close to her ear.

"Yes," she answered, not knowing why she'd been singled out.

"Formerly of the FBI?"

"Yes. But I don't . . ." She was going to say that she didn't understand what her past connection to the FBI had to do with this, but then she didn't complete her sentence. The FBI had obviously had a stake in the first *White Orchid* filming. There was no reason to discount that they would have an interest in the remake.

"I'm afraid we may need your assistance," he said. He looked like he was caught between discomfort and pique. "Could we go into another room to chat? And I have a number for you to call."

"You think this might have an FBI connection, Sheriff?" she asked.

"The FBI seems to think it might."

"But I'm retired."

"The FBI doesn't seem to think that matters." The resentment in his voice could be cut with a knife.

"I didn't ask to be included in anything, Sheriff."

46

"Sorry," he said, somewhat sheepishly, as he turned and indicated which direction they would take from the room to bring as little attention to themselves as possible. Few seemed to notice—except, Charlotte could clearly see, the Air Force colonel, Ed Winslow, and the actor cast in the movie as the FBI inspector, Stephen Taylor. Whenever Charlotte was in the room with that man, he seemed to be studying her—not that Charlotte could legitimately complain; that's exactly what she was here for—to advise him on his role. Or at least up until this moment that's what she had been here for.

Just like that, on the case again, Charlotte thought, as she slipped out a side door in the wake of Sheriff Reynolds.

* * * *

"Hello, beautiful. Just can't keep yourself out of trouble, can you?"

"How did you get onto what's happening down here so quickly, Evan? And what does this have to do with anything in Maryland?"

"I didn't 'get onto' what's happening down there, Charlotte," Evan Worthington, the head of the FBI Annapolis office responded. "It dropped in my lap. Whatever is going on down there rang a bell in the director's office. You know I want you to come back on board as a consultant. This would be a good opportunity for you to do that."

Evan Worthington was one of Charlotte's romantic entanglements from the past when both of them were training at the FBI Academy in Quantico, Virginia. Another woman, now deceased, had come between them then, but Worthington was now the head agent in Charlotte's old office and wanting her back—both in the office and in his life. Part of the reason Charlotte had agreed to come down to Florida was to hold him off, as tempting as he was, because she didn't want anything threatening the life she was building with Brenda.

"What's the director's interest in this—other than John Lu having been involved heavily in the first attempt to film this movie forty years ago? Surely the director hasn't remembered John Lu all this time."

"Apparently he has. That name was mentioned in my conversation with one of his minions. They are sending a file, they say. I don't know what the interest is yet, but I should when I get that file. You're there. You're one of the best investigators we've ever had. When I find out what the director's interest is, are you willing to investigate it? We'll vet you with the local authorities."

"Which might not be too healthy for me," Charlotte said into the phone.

"One of them is standing next to you and scowling, isn't he or she?"

"He. And that would be a yes."

"I could always send Steve Stanton down. He's not you. But he's biting at the bit to get a trip to Florida."

"He should see the size and attitude of the mosquitoes down here. Disney World this isn't."

"So, is that a yes? You'll do whatever legwork down there the director wants done?"

Charlotte paused.

"Maybe I know something that will convince you," Worthington continued. "You didn't ask me what the director's assistant had to say about John Lu when she called."

"Which was what?"

48

"Yesterday, at about the same time your plane went down in Florida, John Lu was murdered in the exercise yard of the prison he was in in California. And I was told that the director worked the John Lu Chinese spy case when John was calling himself Edward Chang. It's just a coincidence, I'm sure, so you might not have much to investigate, but my guess is that's a connection the director wants checked out."

"I'll add Lu's death to the coincidence pile, Evan. We seem to be specializing in those down here. It wasn't on the news, but part of the story down here is that it looks like where the plane went down in the Everglades was very close to where they've found a car connected to the disappearances of the two in the original *White Orchid* film troupe when that broke up. Which is just another coincidence, I guess. But there already are too many coincidences, aren't there?"

"And we never figured out what John Lu was really up to down in Florida that first time, did we?—unless the file they send me tells me a lot more than the director's assistant told me on the telephone. They didn't have enough to make a connection to him then."

"Why did the FBI trot down here in 1972 for a shooting and the disappearance of some film people?"

"I'll check on that, Charlotte. It's a good question. All of your questions are good questions. That's one reason I want you back."

"Just one reason?"

"Yes just one—I think you know that. So, I can hear the wheels spinning in your brain—and your investigative juices flowing. You're going to tell me yes, aren't you?"

"Yes . . . I guess so."

"Thank you." Charlotte could hear the sigh of relief in his voice. "Let me talk to the upstanding man of the law standing up beside you and I'll get the wheels rolling on vetting you as the FBI's agent down there—and give him some sort of idea why the FBI is interested, even though that's not fully clear to me yet. And, Charlotte . . ."

"Yes?"

"I miss you in my life. I can't wait to see you in person again."

"That's nice to hear, Evan," Charlotte said, as she turned the telephone over to Sheriff Reynolds. She couldn't lie and say she wasn't pleased and flattered to hear Evan say that. But she could say that she was pleased and concerned at the same time.

After Sheriff Reynolds had talked with Evan and rung off, he turned and said in a rather flat voice, "I guess that's that, then. We'll say something to those assembled, and then I guess you, Sheriff Gordon, and I will have to put our heads together."

"I didn't ask for this, Sheriff. I'll do my best to keep out of your way on anything that doesn't seem to have an espionage connection with it. The other choice here is for a real agent to come down from Washington."

"Espionage?" he asked, his voice showing his surprise.

"Yes, didn't you know that? The first time they tried to make this film, there were espionage implications, and before the FBI could zero in on that, the filming was stopped and the cast and crew dispersed. And yesterday a man who was a key player in that first filming and who has been uncovered as a Chinese Communist spy was murdered in prison. I think the FBI just wants to be sure there's nothing going on of an espionage nature with this second filming."

The sheriff looked rattled to her.

"Won't it help your investigation to have someone be able to give assurances that this isn't a case with national implications, Sheriff?

How many media hounds do you want running around in this county? As I understood it, it was national news for weeks when the original filming melted down in '72."

"OK, I understand. Thanks," he said. And in a more conciliatory voice than before Charlotte had told him that, he said, "Shall we go into the lounge? Do you want to speak to the people there?"

"Just briefly," Charlotte said, "They'll need to know my role has become more official. And it won't make me popular." Then she told him what she'd say and what she'd appreciate him looking for when she said it.

Sheriff Reynolds took Sheriff Gordon aside when they got back to the lounge. Gordon looked a bit rattled after they'd conversed, but he no longer was scowling at Charlotte either.

When Charlotte was introduced as now being a real, credentialed, FBI consultant on the case and not just a consultant on the movie, she could feel more than half those in the room shrinking away from her and not wanting to look her in the eyes. And when she spoke to them just before the cast and crew dispersed, she simply said, "Since whatever happened with the plane may have broader implications—we of course don't know that yet; we are hoping it doesn't—you should be aware that we will have to conduct full background checks on everyone here. I'm sure none of you have anything to hide . . ." and here Charlotte was so grateful that Brenda had already declared her true relationship to both Tony and herself—not because it made a difference to this case, but because it spared Brenda distress ". . . but we do have to cover all bases."

Afterward, when she was meeting in a conference room with the two sheriffs, she wasn't all that surprised when she was told of those who had reacted most concerned that there would be an intensive background check.

"Did you see how that one guy—the chauffeur, Sam Scarloni— reacted when you mentioned the background checks, Agent Diamond?" Sheriff Reynolds asked when they were alone.

"Yes, he's one I was interested in," Charlotte answered. "And just call me Charlotte—or Ms. Diamond around the others, I guess. I'm no longer an agent. Believe me, this is the soft approach the FBI is taking on this. I'm less than a consultant even to them anymore. I'm just here and it saves them paying someone else to show up and feel like they have to get tangled up in your hair to justify the trip."

"We do appreciate that, Ms. . . . . Charlotte," Sheriff Gordon said. "Scarloni was supposed to be on the plane. He wasn't. That makes him a person of high interest. By the way, what the crash investigators suspect is that one of the fuel lines was cut back in Miami—that the plane simply didn't have fuel enough to get here from there. In the heavy rain and all, the pilot probably didn't have time or opportunity to bring it down safely somewhere, which would be hard to do with a corporate jet anyway."

"Those who were supposed to be on the plane but weren't should be the first ones we have a very serious look see at," Reynolds said. "That's this chauffer, who goes to the head of my list. He looks like a gangster. And then the pretty boy actor, Tony Trice."

"What about that young looker, DeeDee Yance?" Gordon asked.

"Not scheduled to be on the plane. Not supposed to be here at all," Reynolds muttered.

Yeah, Charlotte thought. But talk about motive. She just couldn't forget how fortuitous it was that DeeDee was here and the woman who had been chosen over her for a part in the movie wasn't. "We need to look at them too—and first, probably," she said. "But we also need to look at those who died on the plane. We have to consider that one of them was a target."

"But first those who were supposed to fly but who didn't at the last minute." Gordon threw this one in.

"Yes, you're right," Charlotte agreed. She wasn't actually convinced this was right, but it was too early to be setting herself off against the local authorities.

"But we can discount all of those folks who were here and at the Arcadia airport. They couldn't have been in Miami too," Reynolds said.

"No," Gordon rang in. He said it slowly, and Charlotte knew what he was going to say next, and wasn't surprised when that's what he said. "But just because they weren't in Miami doesn't mean they didn't pay someone to be there in their stead and to sabotage the plane. And it could have been someone we don't even know about, someone not in our scope at all."

"So, a wide-open field," Reynolds said. And he sounded deflated to have to acknowledge their inability to limit the field of suspects.

"There's someone else who you don't know, I'm sure, was in Miami when the plane took off," Charlotte said in a quiet voice. She really hated bringing this up, but she'd been tagged with official responsibility on this, so it couldn't be helped.

Both men turned to her.

"What airport did the jet leave from in Miami?"

"One of the smaller fields corporations use, south of Miami," Gordon answered.

"Would that one be the one in Kendall?" Charlotte asked.

"Yes, why do you ask?"

"Ed Winslow, the military technical adviser on the film. He arrived here late last night. He drove from Miami and told me he had spent the previous night in a hotel near that corporate airport the jet flew out of—the one in Kendall. If he knew the jet was there, he could have had opportunity to sabotage it. He was quite open about telling me that, but if he were a clever killer, he probably would have admitted it off the top because he knew we'd find out eventually on our own anyway."

"Is there anyone we can put on the bottom of the list of suspects?" Reynolds asked, his weariness at everything that needed to be pinned down still showing. "I mean, when I looked out over the crowd when you told them they'd be closely scrutinized, I saw all sorts of sour faces—that guy, Jacks, who's listed as playing a cameraman in the new movie and the guy playing an FBI agent, Taylor, and the script girl and most of the cameramen and set workers. They all looked like they have something to hide."

"They work in the movies," Gordon said, with a bitter laugh. "They're probably all druggies and sex perverts and have something to hide."

"Yes, I think there are a couple of people you can put at the bottom of the list—even lower than me," Charlotte said. "David Runion for one. I think he's genuinely crushed that Jeffery Morris, the makeup stylist was on the plane."

"How so?" Reynolds asked.

"The two of them were a couple," Charlotte said.

"Speaking of sex perverts," Gordon muttered under his breath. Reynolds gave him a cautionary look, and Charlotte looked away so Gordon couldn't see the flash of anger that had crossed her face. She assumed that Reynolds had already figured out her relationship with Brenda and would clue Gordon in on that later.

"Anyone else?" Reynolds quickly asked.

"Yes, now that you mention it," Charlotte said. She'd say it, and they could think what they liked. It didn't change how true it was. "Brenda Brandon can go to the end of the list too. Tony Trice is her son—and I know that she thinks the world of him. She had no idea he wouldn't be on the plane, and she was a basket case thinking he was." Then, to stave off any retorts she might receive about that and questioning of her own objectivity—when she knew damn well she was being completely objective about this—Charlotte steamed ahead.

"Have the bodies on the plane or the one in the car been identified yet? You know the film company was sending a crew down there today to do some filming."

"Nobody's going down there today," Gordon said. "We have the area buttoned down until at least tomorrow. I don't mind them filming the wreckage, but not until the investigators are finished with the site—at least for now—and the bodies have been pulled out."

Billy Ray Gordon was sheriff of Collier County, where the crash site was, so that was a definitive answer to that question.

"And, no, the investigators haven't put their stamp of identity on those in the plane definitively—although they say that the personal documents match up with what they can identify. And the only statement the medical examiner has made on the body in the car was that it was a young woman—and that the body has been there for decades."

So, probably the original White Orchid, Sondra Tran then, Charlotte thought. "Luggage. Was there luggage in the car?"

"A couple of suitcases, I was told," Gordon answered.

"Matching?"

"No ma'am, and there appeared to be clothing for both a man and a woman. Not much, though. The suitcases were larger than needed for just the few clothes in them—both of them."

Sounds like a couple that went off in a rush, Charlotte thought. She moved to a new line of inquiry.

"The pilot. I believe he was the studio's pilot for that plane. I know about the other three, the young actress Dawn James, the makeup artist Jeffery Morris, and the consultant Peter Nguyen. But I know nothing about the pilot."

"He was identified as Larry Chin," Gordon said. "And he was old. Sixty or more. Above the limit for flying commercially."

"Chin?" Charlotte asked. "So, he was Chinese?"

"I think it said Taiwanese on the passport they found in the plane," Gordon answered.

"Taiwanese are Chinese too," Charlotte said. "And he was at least sixty."

She didn't say anything else to the two sheriffs, but her mind was spinning its usual possible web links. Sixty would put him old enough to have connections with the first movie—or, more important, to John Lu. And John Lu was Chinese. And not just Chinese. John Lu had been a Chinese Communist spy.

Chapter five: Vital Connections and In the Still of the Night

"When did the Collier County sheriff say we could go to the crash site?"

"Tomorrow afternoon at the earliest," Charlotte answered. She was somewhat surprised that the question had come from Ed Winslow. It was late afternoon, and the "concept" team for the movie script, basically consisting of the screenwriter Ted Jameson and the technical advisers, Charlotte and Ed Winslow, but this time augmented by the producer, Aaron Woolridge, and the director, Howard Holton, was meeting to try to get a storyline started. Only Holton didn't seem to be frustrated about where they were. He was thinking of all of the footage he could take to play with of the crashed plane and his Jaguar convertible, if the car by the crash scene turned out to be his car, when he could get a film crew in there.

"You seem awfully anxious to get to the crash scene, Ed," Charlotte said.

"I'm a pilot. I admit I can't wait to see the plane and inspect it myself. I might be able to see something that the investigators missed."

"Aaron has told me that you asked for this technical adviser spot—and rather strongly," Charlotte continued. "That they didn't come to you." Her heart had actually sunk when Aaron had told her that. She so didn't want Ed Winslow to be tied up in this in a bad way.

"Yes, I did," he answered, giving Charlotte a level look and what she took to be at least an attempt at a confident smile. "I knew about the original filming at the time. The case had always fascinated me. I wanted to be a part of it."

"Why do I sense that there might be more than that involved?" Charlotte responded. She was pushing him, she knew. She so wanted to be able to put him at the bottom of the suspect list along with David Runion and Brenda.

He didn't give her very much relief on that wish.

"If there is more involved, this isn't the time to tell you, Charlotte. When you've fully decided I'm no longer on your suspect list, let me know. Then we can talk about it. I assure you, though, that whatever deeper interest I have in this, it doesn't involve the sabotage of that plane—at least in any way that would make me a suspect. If there's more, it's that I took an interest in the technical adviser on the early film, General Anderson. He is a very interesting man."

"I have a job to do, Ed. So I'm afraid you'll have to either confide in me or not come off the suspect list until I'm convinced you shouldn't be on it."

"I understand and respect you for that, Charlotte. I wouldn't want to have it any other way."

"Well, yes," Ted Jameson interjected, clearing his throat. "We're here to see if we can get a plotline started. I'm sorry if it's cold-blooded to be concentrating on that rather than on the plane crash, but there it is. Time is money, and we have a movie to make."

An easy stance for you to take, Charlotte thought, as she stopped trying to stare down Ed Winslow and turned back to the rest of the group. Ted could be like the cat catching the canary because of the crash. Before that all he had were longings for David Runion. Now it looked like he had David Runion. That certainly qualified him for the top half of the suspect list for a crash that killed David Runion's lover. He also hadn't even been alive for the original filming—he had no memories to mourn.

"What would be ideal," Holton said, picking up the string, "even more than weaving a plausible plotline, would be solving the mysteries of the original movie and tying them into the current movie we are filming—the movie of a movie production, as it were. If that's my car down there in the Everglades, with Sondra Tran in it, we are presented with the opportunity to build in more realism."

"Can you speak to that, Charlotte?" Woolridge asked. "We've all along seen three original mysteries. The spy angle, with John Lu, the murder of Charlie Teng, and then the disappearance of Sondra Tran, Scott Carr, and Peter Nguyen. The jazzier of the two is the Lu connection, with the disappearance of Sondra and Carr being the romantic element. There is very good material here if we can get control of it."

"Yes, I think you can start with that, Aaron. But what we're missing on the espionage angle is why John Lu was here to begin with. The movie making was only a cover for his spy activities, although we can only assume that in hindsight. He was a spy and he was much too anxious for this movie to be made here. The real mystery there was what brought him here and who he might have been pursuing—or teamed up with."

"Well, he was connected to Sondra, of course."

"He was?" Charlotte rounded on Howard Holton, who had blurted that out.

"Yes, certainly. She was his younger sister. Or least that's what we'd all believed. We knew that family back in Hollywood. At the time, Aaron and I assumed all of this hard push he was making on this movie was to provide his sister with a star vehicle. Isn't that right, Aaron?"

"Yes," Aaron confirmed. "Although he didn't seem to take her disappearance all that seriously. At least it didn't seem to affect him like it did my assistant producer, Phan Van Huy. Huy obviously had a crush on Sondra. He almost fell apart at the suggestion that Sondra and Scott had run off together. It was quite a love triangle thing—and Sondra was egging them both on. There was always the suspicion that Huy had had something to do with the couple's disappearance. Although with Howard's Jag missing the same night, the police leaned toward an elopement."

"Yes, that's right," Howard chimed in.

"Wait a minute," Charlotte said. "Back up there. You say Sondra Tran was John Lu's sister?"

"Yes, of course. I thought everyone knew that," Woolridge answered.

"Well, I didn't," Charlotte said. She wondered what else everyone else supposedly knew that she didn't.

"Well, there's our lead-in right there," Ted Jameson said, visibly pleased. "And it's our connection to the refilming too if that car in the Everglades is Howard's Jaguar and the body is Sondra's. Sondra can have been part of whatever spy thing was going on—Charlotte can either discover that for us in the next few days or we can devise something that will fit—and discovering the car forty years later—especially if there's only one body—opens the door for mysteries reawakening. Dynamite plot opportunities."

"Yes, I can see it," Woolridge said.

"As can I," Holton chimed in. "Charlotte, you're looking pensive."

"There might be at least one more good connection," she said, her face still screwed up in deep thought. They sat there, looking at her expectantly, willing her to come up with something good. "What made you decide to take this movie up again Aaron? Howard?"

"Hmm, let me see," Woolridge considered. "I think we've always had it on a backburner, haven't we, Howard?"

"Yes, quite."

"But it could have stayed on the backburner. Why now?"

"Well, there's always the fortieth year anniversary." Ted Jameson prompted. "I think you said you considered it every ten years. But wasn't it the reappearance of Peter Nguyen, Aaron? Didn't I remember you saying that Peter showed up again wanting a job in the movies forty years after walking out of that original film, where he was cast as the Viet Cong brother of Sondra's character? Wasn't that what set you off? Wasn't Peter the real catalyst for taking the film up again?"

"Yes, that's right, Aaron," Holton interjected. "Peter was so enthusiastic about going back to filming *White Orchid*. And he wanted to be a technical adviser on it."

"He's connected to both periods," Charlotte said. "And now he's dead, killed in a plane sabotaging. How did he account for his disappearance in the first place?"

Aaron answered after a moment of hesitancy, almost as if he were betraying a confidence. "I promised to keep his secret, but I guess he has no need of it now. He said he'd received a warning—that he still had family in Vietnam, and that he received threats against them if he continued with the film. He said he disappeared as much to escape those who had caught up with him from his past as much as to cut out on the film."

"Then perhaps that's what John Lu was doing there," Ted Jameson spoke up. "Maybe Lu was just there to sabotage the making of a film the Air Force wanted made."

"Perhaps," Ed Winslow interjected. "But I'm sure that Charlotte will keep considering the bigger picture. Intimidation seems a rather low-level assignment for Lu, from what I've heard of his importance, and he *was* the one who wanted to make the movie."

"Oh, the possibilities. This is something we can work with." Ted Jameson sounded almost joyous.

Charlotte, though, was now thinking of even another angle, more tenuous than the rest, so she didn't say anything yet. There was the sixty-year-old Chinese pilot of the crashed plane. Old enough to be involved in whatever was happening with John Lu in the original filming—and Chinese enough to have been involved with Lu. And they died on the same day—along with Peter Nguyen.

"I can start writing some scenarios up," Jameson was saying.

"And when we can get out to the crash site, we can check on the car out there and begin shooting the scene," Holton was saying, his voice dreamy, already seeing the images in his mind. "They can start in the opening credits and they also give us an opening scene—the crash that ties today to the past."

"You still want to go down there?" Charlotte turned to Ed Winslow and asked. He'd been very quiet most of time the others were talking, but Charlotte had seen that he had hung on every word and his eyes had been flashing. She couldn't get beyond the suspicion that he knew something that would blow this whole investigation and movie plotline sky high.

"Yes, certainly. I'm chomping at the bit. And you?"

"I wouldn't miss it for the world."

"Well, this certainly has given me an appetite," he said, with a small laugh. "May I escort you to dinner, fair lady?"

"I wouldn't miss that for the world either," Charlotte answered.

He escorted her into the dining room and they sat at "the" table—the one that everyone else revolved around—with Brenda, Tony, DeeDee, Aaron, and Howard. Charlotte wasn't sure that anyone else in the cast and crew wanted to sit anywhere close to her. When she entered the room on the arm of Ed Winslow, all talk had ceased for a split second and then there had been a low-volume buzzing. Everyone seemed to be watching her, but they also seemed to be leaning away from her. Charlotte could almost smell the fear and uncertainty in the room. She no longer was one of them; she was the law.

Neither David Runion nor Ted Jameson appeared at dinner. Charlotte assumed they were taking a private dinner again in David's room. She had never known David to be this reclusive. She was more convinced than ever that the plane crash would not have been any part of his doing. But of Ted Jameson, she wasn't nearly as sure.

That evening, as with the previous evening, Charlotte and Ed conversed comfortably in their own little world as the others slowly peeled off to their own rooms and their own devices. When she finally—and reluctantly, because she found Ed's company so interesting—said her good nights and headed to the suite she now shared with Brenda, she was surprised to spy Tony stealthily climbing the stairs to the second floor of the women's building. DeeDee's room was up there. Charlotte understood sexual desires and agreed that DeeDee was a beautiful young woman—on the outside. But, like Brenda, for the life of her, Charlotte couldn't understand why a fine young man like Tony couldn't see through to the spoiled brat and user inside that woman.

* * * *

He had waited, hidden, in the closet of the suite's living room for what seemed to be hours, waiting for her to settle in the other room—the bedroom. This would bring unwanted attention, but it was too late for that already. The place already was crawling with cops. But it had to be done.

He listened for signs that she was still stirring, but he heard nothing. He opened the closet door a crack. The door into the bedroom was in his line of sight. It was ajar. No light was showing through from the other room. He crept out of the closet and up to the door, listening intently. He could hear her breathing. It seemed to sound regular

65

enough to signify that she was asleep already. Still he stood there, waiting.

It was perhaps a good twenty minutes later before he slid into the bedroom. He knew where everything was because he had checked the room out earlier. He'd left the drapes on the window slightly open so that there would be enough light in the room for him to maneuver. She hadn't pulled them to. Shortly after she'd come into the suite—in the living room, where he was hiding in the closet—a knock on the door had announced the appearance of the man. They'd argued briefly. Although the voices were muffled enough that he couldn't follow the conversion, she'd sounded like a real bitch, although he never lifted his voice. It was strange that the woman could act that way. It certainly wasn't how she came across in public. As soon as she was alone again she'd gone into the bedroom—and then the bath, where she'd spent a god awful lot of time primping herself. Then straight to bed . . . and, it appeared into a sound sleep.

This would be easier than he'd thought. He'd thought the bitch would read for hours and then be a light sleeper. It was her vigilance he was worried about. But she'd gone right off to sleep.

He moved as noiselessly as he could toward the bed. He was holding the sofa pillow he'd brought from the sofa in the small living room in a tight grip with both of his gloved hands.

He was standing over her now, looking down at her in the dimness created by what little light was coming through the slightly open drapes. He heard the sound of an airplane overhead. Flying low, flying close. He was afraid that it might startle her awake. But no bother if it did. He already was here, in place. In fact, she had an arm slung across her face that would need to move for him to get this pillow firmly over her face.

"Hey, bitch." he said, none too softly.

The arm moved away, and her eyes popped open in a jarring look of surprise and fear.

* * * *

"Wake up, Brenda. Did you hear that? That was no dream."

"Yes, I'm awake. I heard it too. Or them."

"A plane landing. Gunshots. Sounded like automatic weapons fire. And a plane taking off again," Charlotte said.

"Yes, exactly."

"Better go—" But Charlotte hadn't gotten any farther than moving the covers off her legs when the start of a blood-curdling scream—right here in the woman's building—rose to a crescendo.

Now Brenda was springing from the bed too, babbling and completely at a loss for her usual calm restraint.

"No, Brenda. I'll go. Call someone over in the men's building, please. Tell them we need help over here."

The women's building was smaller, if plushier, than the men's was, because there weren't as many women working on the movie. There were two suites and two double rooms and the large lounge on the first floor, and two suites and six double rooms on the second. Brenda's suite was the one on the first floor corner, overlooking the landing strip. The dining room workers and domestic staff were housed in another building altogether. The women assigned to this building were just Claire Yang, the actress playing White Orchid in the new

67

filming, the script girl; and a few secretaries, one of the camera operators, and a group of costumers and makeup artists; in addition to Brenda and Charlotte. And now there was DeeDee Yance too, in Charlotte's former suite on the upper floor, directly above Brenda's.

All of the women were out in the hall and moving toward the suite above Brenda's when Charlotte got up to the second floor. Being trained to observe, she quickly indentified everyone who was there and what they were clothed in, how close they were to the end of the hall, and how awake and surprised and concerned each appeared to be. She also saw that the window at the end of the hall was gaping open—and she already knew that it looked out on a fire escape stairway that gave quick access to the ground. The women who had appeared were clumped together in the hallway and clinging to each other in fright—all except for one woman standing near the far end of the hallway.

"In here," Claire Yang was crying out. She was in a negligee, tightly held to her body, with, Charlotte could tell, nothing underneath. She was standing in the open living room door to the suite above Brenda's. Claire's suite was directly across the hall from that one, so it didn't surprise Charlotte that Claire was the first one there. It also didn't surprise Charlotte that much that she got a glimpse of a near-naked man moving back into the interior of Claire's suite beyond her open doorway. That would probably be Clifford Boyd, Charlotte registered in her thoughts. She'd seen the vibes going back and forth between those two for days.

"I was afraid to go in by myself," Claire said in a breathy voice as Charlotte approached her. All of the other women advanced down the hall, huddled defensively behind Charlotte's authoritative and formidable body.

"Good choice. I'll go in first. You might want to wait for the men to arrive from the other building, though. And maybe go back in your suite and put more clothes on. Cliff too."

Claire blushed and retreated back into her suite.

The screaming continued, so Charlotte surmised that the actual danger had already escaped through the window at the end of the hall and that DeeDee must not be mortally wounded if she still was able to exercise her lungs so heartily.

"Shush, DeeDee, you're safe now," Charlotte said, perhaps a bit more harshly than she would for another woman, as she entered the bedroom.

She switched on the lights. DeeDee was sitting up in bed, the covers clutched up to beneath her chin.

"A man. He had a pillow. He was going to smother—"

"Yes, yes. You're safe. It's all over now, DeeDee," Charlotte said more soothingly. She could kick herself. DeeDee had every right to be hysterical. "Did you recognize who it was? What made him stop?"

She saw the sofa pillow on the floor by the bed, so she didn't really need DeeDee to give her any more explanation of what had almost happened here. Unfortunately, she also didn't need an explanation of why he had stopped. She'd ask for the pillow to be dusted for prints—and other areas of the suite, but she had no doubt he'd worn gloves.

"A plane. I heard a plane. That half woke me up. Then I heard him, and I opened my eyes. And I just screamed. I didn't really see him . . . it was too dark . . . but he called me a bitch . . ."

Charlotte almost cracked a smile at that.

". . . and then I screamed . . . and he was gone."

At that point the room was suddenly filled with men in various versions of nightclothes. A somewhat red-faced Clifford Boyd was leading the pack, but Aaron Wooldridge, Ed Winslow, Tony, and Howard Holton were close behind. Cameron Jacks, the actor playing the role in the refilming of the cameraman who ran off with White Orchid; Ted Jameson; and Sam Scarloni, the chauffeur, were in the background. Charlotte quickly registered that David Runion wasn't there. She assumed that Ted would be able to vouch for where David was ten minutes earlier, though. She saw that a few other men were missing too, but from the pitch of the voices out in the hallway, she assumed that some were still out there chatting up the half-clad women gathered in the hall.

"Ms. Yance has been attacked—by a man, she said. Perhaps you men could search this building and the others and account for everyone." She was looking at Ed Winslow. She didn't know why, other than instinctively thinking that he was the sharpest and most collected of those present, and he was the one who answered.

"Yes, certainly. I'll take a group and go back to the men's building. Clifford, perhaps you could take some men and search the main building. Tony, maybe the staff building? Aaron, you and Howard, this one?"

No one questioned his authority or his assignments. They all quickly went out into the hallway to divvy up the search teams.

Brenda had arrived and had taken up Charlotte's station, sitting on the bed and comforting DeeDee. Charlotte was greatly relieved to be rescued from performing that task. She followed the men out into the hallway.

"A word, please, Tony," she called out, "before you go, please."

Tony drew aside with Charlotte. A questioning look was painted on his face.

"I noticed you didn't rush to DeeDee's side, Tony. I would have thought—"

"We've had a falling out, Charlotte. I didn't think I could comfort her under the circumstances."

"And yet I saw you creeping up the stairs to this floor as I was coming to bed. You weren't going to comfort DeeDee then?"

He looked downcast and sheepish. "That was when we had our falling out. I'd come to her suite to tell her there wasn't anything left in us any more. We did fight. But, I swear, Charlotte, that she was still very much awake and not prepared for bed when I left her."

"Well, I'm glad to hear you've come to your senses on that young woman at least. What time did you leave?"

"Not more than an hour ago. Not that long, really, before she must have been attacked. And she locked the door behind me. I heard it click."

"Then he probably was in the suite while you were there—that broadens the time frame that suspects will have to account for. Unless he came in through a window. He left via the hall window, I'm quite sure. But if the door to the suite was locked, and if he came in through a window, it would have to be one of the ones in her living room or bedroom. We'll have to check."

"I'm sorry, Charlotte."

"No, don't be. You've helped establish a few things. And, don't worry, DeeDee didn't even hint that it might have been you who assaulted her. Now go on, take your search party. And let me know what you find."

71

As she watched him go, she breathed a sigh of relief—not only because he finally had come to his senses about his relationship with DeeDee Yance, but also because the young actress might have thought it advantageous for her to take out her vengeance on him, given this opportunity, but she hadn't. Charlotte would have considered such behavior quite likely from the young woman.

When she reentered the suite, it was to hear Brenda offering DeeDee refuge.

"If you are too afraid to be alone here, we could ask one of the makeup girls to take the sofa in the living room—it's a sofa bed. Or better yet, you could come downstairs and sleep on the sofa bed in our rooms."

She looked up at Charlotte. "That would be fine with us, wouldn't it, Charlotte? At least for tonight?"

Oh, lordy, is what Charlotte thought. But what she actually answered, turning her head away so that neither of the women on the bed could see her facial expression was, "Yes, that would be just peachy."

The men were back shortly. "All accounted for but the guy playing the FBI agent in the new movie, Stephen Taylor," Ed Winslow reported. "Should we search the grounds too?"

"No, it's too dark out, and everyone needs to get back to bed," Charlotte said. "Just, everyone lock up the buildings tight when you're all in, do another internal search after you lock up, and then go back to bed. If Sam's our culprit, he deserves to have to spend the night outside."

Later, when Brenda had gotten a simpering DeeDee, now playing the role for all it was worth, bedded down on the sofa bed in the living room to their suite, she entered the bedroom and gave Charlotte a very concerned look.

"Charlotte, that room . . . DeeDee . . ."

"I know," Charlotte answered. "I know that wasn't supposed to be DeeDee's room . . . that there was no reason for anyone to know that it wasn't me in that bed. I'm fully aware of that. But we'll think about that in the morning. And we'll think about that airplane that touched down and those gun shots in the morning as well. The attack on DeeDee may have driven that out of everyone else's minds—but not mine. But it's all something better faced in the morning. Come to bed now. I'm jealous of the comforting you've been giving DeeDee. I want some comforting given me too."

"Much more willingly, I can assure you," Brenda answered.

"The evening's good news is that Tony told me that it's finally off between him and DeeDee."

"The best news I've gotten today," Brenda answered, as the two climbed back into bed.

Chapter Six: Into the Everglades

"It's just a short hop from here to Colombia in a small plane. Even shorter to Cuba. Not far at all to Cuba. And we've never been able to do much about interdicting the small-plane traffic in Florida from the Caribbean and South America."

Ed Winslow had been giving Charlotte what she took to be a meaningful look when he said that, maybe more meaningful than the obvious. The two of them, along with Sheriff Roy Reynolds of DeSoto County, were gathered around a sheet-covered body on the tarmac at Carlstrom Field. A deputy sheriff had just walked up to them to report on what had been found in Stephen Taylor's room in the men's building.

"A whole lot of cash and a whole lot of packaged white powder in that room, Sheriff," he'd said. "We sent both back to the lab."

"Not surprised," the sheriff answered tersely. "Have Sadie put in a call to the DEA office. After that track down that guy I wanted to interview further and have them empty a conference room where I can talk to him."

"Well, that complicates matters more," Sheriff Reynolds said when the deputy had walked briskly back toward the main building. Then he sighed. "Guess I won't be going down to the Everglades with you folks this afternoon. I'll try to spring loose a couple of deputies to go with you. We'll, make sure the lab gets fingerprints off the body and that empty satchel under the body there. We ran a blank going not too far back on investigating this dude. So, it doesn't surprise me that he had some reason to be here other than the film."

He then turned to Charlotte and Ed. "Who found the body? And what's this about one of the women being assaulted here last night?"

"I found the body," Winslow said. "We were going to search for Taylor—or whoever he really is—this morning because he was the only one not accounted for when we checked after Ms. Yance was attacked last night. But I'm an early riser and like to walk before breakfast. So, I was out before the others. The body wasn't hard to see; it was right out here on the runway."

"It does look like the body's been here for a while, but I'll wait on that until the medical examiner has his say." The sheriff said that in his "don't leave town without telling me" voice while he was staring pretty hard at Ed.

"But I'm afraid there's no connection between what happened here—and Stephen Taylor—and the attack on DeeDee," Charlotte said.

"How do you figure that?" the sheriff asked. "Winslow here says you were looking for Taylor in connection with the attack."

"We heard the gunshots that killed Taylor last night—or at least Brenda Brandon and I did—and that was just seconds before DeeDee managed to foil her attacker by screaming. Taylor couldn't have been attacking her while he was being killed out here. And it won't take a medical examiner to determine that he died from gunshot wounds. Several shots. It was automatic weapons fire that I heard."

"Anyone else hear it?"

"When I asked folks if they had, some of them seemed to think they might have, but I can't say it wasn't by power of suggestion. The women's building is closer to the airstrip than the men's building and our room is on the corner facing here."

"Our room?"

"Yes, Brenda Brandon and I are sharing a suite now."

"Oh, I see."

"DeeDee Yance arrived unexpectedly, and I gave her my suite—the one above Brenda's—and moved in with Brenda. But that wasn't general knowledge."

Reynolds chomped on the inference of that for a moment before responding. "OK, I understand."

"Are you sure you understand, Sheriff?" Charlotte added.

Reynolds had a pained expression as if he was irritated that Charlotte was rubbing in her relationship with Brenda, but Charlotte quickly put him out of any misery he was having on that point. "The significance of that, I think, is that the attacker most likely didn't think he was attacking DeeDee. Chances are very good he thought he was attacking me. And not just attacking. He was going to smother his victim with a pillow."

"Oh, now I do see," Reynolds quickly said. "So, you think it was someone who didn't like you being assigned to the investigation?"

"It looks that way," Charlotte answered.

"And it wasn't Taylor," Ed Winslow muttered. "So, whoever it was is still among us."

"Did you hear the gunshots, Mr. Winslow?" the sheriff asked.

"No, I can't say I did. Or Ms. Yance screaming—or anything else before I walked back into my bedroom from the bathroom. I was in the shower when the alarm was raised on the attack on her." He turned toward Charlotte. "I'm distressed to hear that you were supposed to be in that room. We'll have to see that someone sticks close to you until this is all settled. I feel like I shouldn't let you out of my sight now."

Charlotte almost blushed at that. She looked away to see that the people who had been gathered by the buildings and watching the activity around the body on the runway, accompanied by a great deal of animated conversation, were mostly gone now. Not dispersing, however, was a small group at a patio table outside of the doors into the main building's buffet room. She could make out Brenda. And David Runion sitting there, with Ted Jameson hovering over him. But there was another man—not from the film company—fussing over David too. Charlotte wanted to be in two places at once. But she was here, with the sheriff now, and there were other matters to be discussed.

"It wasn't just the gunshots and DeeDee's screams that woke us last night, Roy. A plane touched down, then the gunshots, and then it took right back off again. And this isn't the first time we heard a plane come in here at night. I'm sure now that one came in the previous night, too, but Brenda and I both marked that up to nightmares connected to the plane crash in the Everglades."

That was the point at which Ed Winslow had interjected the thought of how frequently small planes from foreign climes to the south were sneaking into Florida undetected by coastal defenses.

"No doubt Taylor was a drug runner middle man, using the filming at an abandoned airstrip as a cover for being down here," Reynolds said. "They were using this landing strip for their exchanges, and might have been doing so before the film company took it over. Guess they had a falling out of the clan."

"You said you couldn't trace him very far back in the background check," Charlotte said.

"Yes, I was going to come back out here today anyway. A couple of the people out here have shallow pasts, and I wanted to get some fingerprinting done—mostly the cameramen, and the actor playing a cameraman in the film, Cameron Jacks, and the actress Claire Young. That can't be her real name. That one only pops up earlier this year."

"You, of course, are squeaky clean, Winslow," he said to Ed. "A genuine air ace, we found. And your brother before you too. Quite the heroes, although too bad about your brother—going down on his last mission in Nam like that. But not a drop of bad news on you, there wasn't."

Without waiting for either Ed or Charlotte to say anything about that, the sheriff continued down his list. "And there was the Taylor guy. I want to work up the chauffeur, Sam Scarloni. Now there may be a real piece of work. We can go back only so far on him, but we've traced back far enough to put him in a compound with a bunch of macho, anti-everything weekend warriors called the Minuteman Advance organization. Either of you know what he was up to with that?"

"Not me," Charlotte said, as Ed shook his head as well. "I haven't really been near enough to him to discuss backgrounds." Ed was looking pensive, and Charlotte thought he was thinking of saying something. But he didn't.

The medical examiner and an ambulance with attendants arrived at that moment. The sheriff made introductions all around, and Charlotte and Ed both briefly filled the medical examiner in on what they knew about Taylor's bullet-riddled body being out on the airstrip. At the tail end of this, the deputy sheriff was returning, and when Charlotte looked around at hearing his approach, she saw that the group of her colleagues and the man she didn't know were still huddled at the patio table back at the main building.

"Can't find the Scarloni guy anywhere, Sheriff," the deputy said as he approached them. "And the production manager guy says there's a company SUV missing too. Should we put the license plate number out over the airwaves?"

"Chrise' almighty, it don't just rain, it pours around here," Sheriff Reynolds exclaimed. "Damn right we put out an APB on him— and search again, in case he's still here and just doesn't want to be found."

"If I'm not needed here anymore, sheriff—" Charlotte said.

"No," the sheriff answered, "I know you gotta get ready for the trip down to the Everglades. Just leave your cell phone number with the detective sitting at the reception desk. I'll call you if anything else comes up—which, considering all that's already happened—will probably be in about ten minutes."

Charlotte turned and walked toward her friends on the patio. Ed Winslow fell into step behind her. As they reached the patio, though, he hung back a bit, but still within hearing distance.

The stranger was talking to David Runion. "Can you tell me what you had for breakfast, Mr. Runion?"

"Eggs . . ."

"Scrambled," Ted Jameson offered. The stranger gave Ted a slightly perturbed look, and the screenwriter stopped hovering quite so close over Runion and clamped his jaw shut.

"And what else?"

"A muffin and coffee and orange juice. I think. That's right, isn't it, Ted?" Charlotte noted a hesitancy and slight slurring of David's words. Runion was looking at Jameson, who had a sad expression on his face. He nodded. Charlotte could tell it was a strain for him not to speak for David.

"And who is the president?" the stranger, who Charlotte had now figured out was a doctor, asked.

"Sydney Craxton."

The doctor looked up at Jameson with a questioning look on his face, but it was Brenda who answered.

"Sydney is the president of the movie studio. The studio is David's life. I doubt he could tell you who the president of the United States was on his best day—and it hasn't been more than six weeks since David's been a guest at the White House." Her voice was shaky and revealed her concern as well.

David was swiveling his head around, taking in everyone within fifty feet in a separate, determined, slow effort to identify each one and pull him or her into his realm of reality.

"He was such a gorgeous man. I think maybe my first crush. But, no of course, not, but the first one I wanted and who didn't want me."

"Who, Mr. Runion? Who are you talking about?" The question was from the doctor.

"I wanted him, but he wanted the orchid—and so did Huy. God, that man had a temper. And . . ." David laughed here, ". . . the orchid kept brushing up to me. She just didn't know. A love foursome, was that? So much more complicated than a love triangle, wouldn't you think? And in the end . . ."

"He who?" Ted blurted, not being able to hold back. "Who was the 'him' you wanted."

"Ted, I don't think now . . . He's talking about the past. Our first filming here, Doctor. Those were people here at the time." This had been interjected by Brenda, who was looking quite distressed now.

"Scott. Scott Carr. Such a beautiful young man. And wasted on her. I don't know where they . . ."

Runion just stopped talking at that point and withdrew into himself.

"I'm sorry I waited," Ted murmured. "I thought he might come out of it—that it was just a temporary shock from the plane crash."

"And that's why we haven't seen much of David since the crash?" Charlotte asked. "You've been keeping him back, hoping he'd come out of it and there'd be no complications with the filming?"

Jameson lowered his eyes, perhaps misunderstanding censure in Charlotte's voice. But she could see that he had been doing what David would have wanted. It was Brenda who put it into words, though. She reached over and put a comforting hand on Ted's arm.

"We all know that David would approve—that he'd do anything to keep the show going. And, as I said, the movies are his life.

81

You did call in a doctor this morning. I know that must have been a difficult decision."

"There's an ambulance out front," the doctor said. "We'll take him to the hospital. A very private room, I promise. The media won't know he's there. We'll check him out, but I'd say that he's probably had a mild stroke—brought on, no doubt, by the loss of his friend in this plane crash you told me about. In many cases, the patient comes out of it and fully regains his faculties. Don't worry, we'll give him the best of care."

"I'll go inform those who need to know," Brenda said. She leaned down and gave David a kiss on the forehead and he looked up and said, "Don't fret, Susan, there will always be tomorrow."

Tears came into Brenda's eyes, as the doctor and Ted helped David rise from the patio chair and move into the main building.

"Susan?" Charlotte asked.

"That was the last line he spoke to my character in a movie we filmed a good thirty years ago," Brenda whispered. "His only Academy Award nomination." And then she was gone as well, swallowed up by the main building, but replaced by the figure of one of the movie company's secretaries walking out onto the patio.

"Ms. Diamond, there's a long-distance call for you. Mr. Woolridge said you'd probably want to take it in his office."

Charlotte started into the building but sensed more than saw that Ed Winslow had fallen into step behind her.

"I know how to answer a telephone by myself," she said, with a laugh meant to lighten but not dismiss her statement.

"I won't come into the office with you," he answered. "But I'll be right outside the door. I was serious that you shouldn't be on your own until we find and stop whoever meant to attack you last night."

Charlotte gave him a sour look, but she secretly was pleased. She enjoyed Ed's company, and he was the type of man one just couldn't remain indifferent to. Inside she picked up the telephone receiver and was put through directly to Evan Worthington in Annapolis.

"So, you must have received the file from the director?" she said, hoping that he wasn't calling because he'd already heard about the shooting of the suspected drug runner. If the case got any more complicated, Charlotte was afraid he'd be sending the agent, Steve Stanton, down here for real, and Charlotte didn't want him in her hair.

"Yes, and I can see his concern. The spy ring down there during the first filming was much more extensive than just John Lu."

"The missing actress, Sondra Tran too?"

"Yes, how did you know?"

"I just yesterday found out she was John Lu's sister."

"Not just her, though. Phan Van Huy, the assistant producer and Peter Nguyen, who played the actress's brother in the film. Both of them were connected to Lu. The murder victim, Charlie Teng, the company's plane pilot too. Charlotte, whatever was going on down there at the time was big. Very big."

"I still don't understand what brought the FBI into it in 1972. I understand that John Lu was on the radar, but not anything to the extent that we later found out, was he?"

"That's in the file," Worthington answered. "Signals intercepts pinned down traffic between the film location and the PRC embassy in

Washington, D.C. Before that Lu was just a suspect, it was at that point, with a high level of clandestine radio traffic, that the FBI stepped up its interest. And it's interest was enhanced by the presence of Thomas Anderson down there?"

"Anderson?"

"Yes, he'd been sent down to Florida more or less on a breather by the Air Force. But he had a team of strategists with him, and he was still heavily involved in planning the U.S. air war in Vietnam. The FBI was afraid that something was laid on concerning him. They shut the film down, but their major interest was in pulling the general out of there."

"Evan, I think the espionage angle is the key to this whole thing," Charlotte said. "Not just to a legal case—but to the plotline for this new movie they want to make. So, where's Phan Van Huy now? He's the only one left not accounted for."

"He's dead. He died in a fall from a hotel balcony in Miami—several weeks after the original filming was broken up. That was ruled an accident, a case of too much booze and too little equilibrium. We'll take another look at that file. But his wife, Rose, was how we got a handle on this to begin with—when we first started tracing what Lu was up to. She was part of the ring, but was down in Key West. We first rolled her up for being in contact with the Cubans. Then we got her to confess her involvement with her husband and Lu, but we never could get out of her what the operation was. There's a good chance she never knew. But there's a chance she did. She may be our best lead at the moment."

"Yeah, if we knew where she was."

"We do. She's down there near you. She's been held in Florida prisons this whole time. She's at the Homestead Correctional Institution near Miami."

"And you think I should talk to her about this again?"

"It's been forty years. She may be ready to talk, yes, and something may be happening again. We can send—"

"No, I'll do it. I'll get over there somehow. Send my credentials down to the prison, please. I'll try to fit it in sometime in the next few days. But there are some leads here to follow up."

Please, please, Charlotte thought, don't ask me what's happening down here. I'm not ready for you to send me yet another bodyguard—and I have the sinking feeling that you would do so.

"I'm still trying to figure out what set this off now," she said.

"I think I have the answer to that, Charlotte. This spy team member, Peter Nguyen. He disappeared forty years ago and then he turned up again. His reappearance could have been the catalyst for something."

"That makes sense," Charlotte said. "Woolridge and Holton both told me that he was the one pressing them to refilm the movie. But he's dead, in the plane crash."

"Right. Which could mean that whatever was supposed to reignite has been snuffed out by accident—or it could mean, since he died in the plane crash, that it was purposely snuffed out by someone who was threatened by it starting up again."

"We're going down to the plane crash site this afternoon," Charlotte said. "There probably isn't anything to be seen down there, but it doesn't hurt to look. I wonder where he's been all these years"

"I have the answer to that too. He's been in Cuba."

"Cuba?" Suddenly Cuba was cropping up here and there. And what had Ed said earlier?—that it was just a short, relatively safe hop from Cuba to here. And, therefore, from here to Cuba as well. Food for thought.

"That's about all I know at the moment," Evan said. "It's good you're down there. The director is all over this. So, I'll let you get to—"

"Just one more thing, Evan. It's looking like the company chauffeur down here, going by the name Sam Scarloni, may be mixed up in this. He was in Miami, was supposed to be on the plane, but wasn't, and now he's missing from here." Charlotte stopped short of saying he might also have tried to murder her the previous night. "And a background check has connected him with some rightist mercenary group called the Minuteman Advance. Do you—?"

"I'll get back to you on that," Evan cut in. His words were clipped and sharp.

"Evan? Something wrong?"

"Maybe. If so, it's too big to bring up without pinning a whole lot down. But I'll get back to you on that as soon as I can."

"You look pensive," Ed said when Charlotte had rung off and walked out of Woolridge's office. "Bad news?"

"No, not really. Just that I seem to need to be in two places at one time. Here and somewhere near Miami. And I really don't want to be gone from here long enough for a two-day trip to Miami."

"Ah, well, then, perhaps I can offer you a ride tomorrow?"

"The company has plenty of drivers—when I can break away for two days. Tomorrow isn't—"

"But do the company driver's have a pilot's license? I do, and we can rent an airplane in Arcadia and be in Miami and back in one day. Tomorrow, if you like."

"You're being awfully helpful to me."

"As I intend to be. I couldn't be happier than if you got to the bottom of what is happening here. So, is that a yes I hear?"

"Yes, of course," Charlotte answered. Ed indeed was bending over backward to help her—almost to the point, she felt again, that he was leading her. Well, OK, if he wanted to stay close to her, she wanted to stay close to him now just as much.

"The cars await outside for your Everglades excursion. Shall we?"

"Lead on MacDuff," Charlotte said. Hand and hand into the cauldron, she thought, perhaps not for the reasons you'd think.

* * * *

The SUVs they were in could only go so far into the Everglades. They were following an old fire trail, and when that gave out, long before they reached the downed plane, they continued on foot until they reached where the old Jaguar roadster had been driven off the side of the trail and had sunk, nose deep and tail raised, into a marshy area.

Four of them, plus a filming crew, had gone with the party from the Collier County police, led by Sheriff Billy Ray Gordon. Charlotte was there because this whole trip at this point was primarily to give the FBI its access to the site. And Ed Winslow was there at his request and because he was an airplane expert, and Sheriff Gordon would be more comfortable if he too found and pointed to the sliced fuel line as the probable cause of the crash. And Howard Holton, the film director, was along partly because he was antsy to get that film footage so that he could get started working on the new film and partly because the missing Jaguar had been his car. If he could identify it, they'd have part of their mystery pinned down, if not solved. Tony was supposedly along to gain the "atmospherics" of the scene to help him with his part in the movie, but he was really there because Brenda asked him to stay close to Charlotte and help keep her safe.

They'd all had to wear trousers tucked into high-topped boots, long-sleeved shirts, gloves, and broad-brimmed hats covered with netting, because the mosquitoes out here in the Everglades were big enough to carry a small dog off. Charlotte had had to borrow what she was wearing from Holton. Woolridge had volunteered his clothes but the embarrassment was that he was just too small. Only Holton had the height and girth to be of use to Charlotte.

After getting out of the SUVs, they'd walked for a couple of miles on a double-tracked road and then for a couple of more miles through underbrush, keeping a careful watch underfoot for signs of the track, and, although no one would say it, for poisonous snakes.

Charlotte saw the bashed-in tail end of the two-seater convertible first when they'd veered off the trail over a sagging stretch of yellow crime-scene tape. One had to have been looking for the rusting, moss-covered vehicle to see it. The party searching for the downed airplane had literally stumbled into it on their way into the jungle, guided by the slashed and burned swatch they could see through the tree canopy marking where the jet had come to ground.

"It's practically rusted through," Charlotte said. When they'd reached the back of the vehicle and both Howard and Ed had just stood there, each deep in whatever thoughts he had, both quite somber. "How could anyone even tell it had once been a lavender car?" she asked no one in particular.

Tony was walking the edges where the land dipped into swamp, checking this and that, almost sniffing the air like a hunting dog.

"Some of the paint inside the trunk was in pretty good shape still," Gordon answered her. "The two suitcases were jammed up against the sides and sealed the space between them and the wall pretty well. Not much trunk space. The two suitcases had taken it all. And there's no backseat."

The four of them shifted around to the side of the vehicle as the cameramen started setting up their shot angles.

"Well?" Gordon asked Holton.

"It could be mine." He wasn't talking directly to Gordon, however. He, like Charlotte and Ed, was devoting his full attention now to the skeleton in the passenger seat.

"We'll be taking her away today," the sheriff said. "The medical examiner determined it was a woman. And there's a bullet hole in the back of her head. She was a mere slip of a girl."

"Yes, if it's Sondra, she'd be a mere slip of a girl." Holton spoke softly, almost reverently.

It wasn't Holton Charlotte was watching out of the corner of her eye. It was Ed Winslow. He had placed his hand tentatively on the top of the door frame on the driver's side and had his head bowed, almost as if in prayer. Charlotte saw what she thought were a few teardrops roll down his cheek.

"Ed?" she said. And then a little louder, "Ed."

"Sorry," he murmured. "All of this time out here, alone. But it's peaceful out here, and a beautiful resting place, in its own way."

"We found these tatterings of paper and leather in the glove compartment," Gordon was holding out a few transparent plastic bags, with fragments in them. "And this key chain, with keys."

"Yes, those are—were—mine," Howard said with a dull voice. "The keys were to a beach house I'd rented in Sarasota for when I wanted to get away from the movie filming. So, I guess it's my car all right. But it's got a big dent in the trunk. If it came in nose first, it shouldn't have gotten that dent, should it? My car was in pristine shape when it disappeared."

"We figure it was rammed off the road from behind," Gordon said in a low voice.

"Yes, I guess it could have been dented from something like that," Holton agreed.

They stood in silence, and then Holton became all business, giving instructions to his film crew on what film footage he wanted of the scene. Tony came back to the group to help the cameramen set up.

Gordon gave the director over thirty minutes to take the film, but the mosquitoes were getting to him—they were getting to everyone—and there was an ominous splashing noise off in the swampy area that reminded them that they weren't alone. The sheriff eventually said that if they were going to have time to inspect the site of the plane crash, they'd best be going. Holton pretty much pretended he didn't hear Gordon until the sheriff noted that time spent here filming was time not available at the crash scene for filming, and that got Holton and his crew motivated to move on.

They were the lucky ones. The original search party had had to move farther into the muck and swamp from the side of the trail on foot. Since they had been there, a crew had laid a four-plank-wide plank bridge on cinderblocks, which made the going a lot easier for Charlotte and the others.

"Yep, that's her. That's one of our company planes," Holton said, as soon as they entered the clearing the burning plane had made. Their noses had been assailed with the stench of tragedy and death well before they could do more than see that something had mashed the jungle in the direction in which they were trudging.

"How can you be—?" Charlotte started to say, but she stopped when she too saw what Holton had seen. Emblazoned on the fuselage of the plane, charred, but still readable, was the name "Brenda."

"Does Brenda know her name is on the plane?" she asked.

"I doubt it. We bought it after she and you left Hollywood last year."

"Then I suggest we not tell her," Charlotte said.

"Agreed."

"The bodies—four of them—were in pretty bad shape," Gordon said. "So, there's nothing for you to try to identify. The lab is working on them and also examining whatever else we could get out of the wreckage. It's pretty well cleared out now. So, if your man from the Air Force wants to do his own investigation, I suggest you make it quick. And the same for the camera works. We want to be in the vehicles and out of the Everglades before dark."

Ed crawled around in the wreckage, doing his best to keep out of the camera shots and came back with the same preliminary verdict the crash investigators had. "It looks burned," he said, "but it's not as badly mangled as it looks. If there had still been the fuel in the plane needed to get from here into Carlstrom Field, there wouldn't have been much fuselage left here from a crash. And I found a fuel line to one of the tanks had been sliced by a sharp knife several times. I would have written the cause of this crash up as suspicious too."

As the film crew was wrapping up its take, Charlotte put a hand on Holton's sleeve.

"Umm, Howard."

"Don't worry, Charlotte, all evidence of the plane's name will be airbrushed out in the first cut at the film."

"Thanks. It would be especially painful for her, I think, because Tony was supposed to be in the plane."

On the way out, Ed Winslow lagged back for a few minutes, alone, at the side of the Jaguar. And he was unusually quiet for the entire ride back to the base camp.

Chapter Seven: The Fast, Nail-biter Trip

"Isn't this one a little beat up? How about that one over there?"

"This one? Why the Cessna 172 is the workhorse of the small plane fleet," Ed Winslow answered Charlotte. They were standing on the tarmac of the Arcadia municipal airport, waiting for Brenda to return from the ladies' room. Brenda had been visibly pleased that Charlotte had asked her if she wanted to join in on the trip to the Miami area.

"Yes, I'd love to," she'd said. "I'm bored stiff waiting around here for Ted to produce even the outline of a script that I can start working on. The sketchy one Tony and I'd been given back in Maryland isn't anything like what he now says is forming up."

Charlotte didn't want to have to tell Brenda that nothing was forming up on a plotline for the movie yet—and wouldn't until they could provide a key motivation for it. Perhaps that would come out of this trip to the Homestead Correctional Institution to interview Rose Phan. But Brenda had snapped up the offer of the excursion so quickly that it made Charlotte reflect on the last couple of days and on how little time she'd spent with Brenda. What Charlotte remembered the most of the past two days was her discussions with Ed Winslow. She certainly hoped that Brenda wasn't feeling shunted aside. Charlotte had no interest in Ed Winslow.

But was that really true? She'd have to give that some thought—the very next time she was given time to think about anything but this case.

"And that plane over there might look new and sleek . . ." Winslow was saying. Then he paused. "Well, it is newer and sleeker than the 172 even though its title indicates otherwise. It's the Cessna 162. But it only has two seats."

At this point Charlotte got the impression that Ed was trying to make sure she was paying attention to him. She wondered if it was a ding for her having invited Brenda to join them on the trip without consulting with him. If so, that was tough, she thought. "And it's a controversial model."

"Oh, how so?"

"It's a relatively new model but it's been manufactured in China. There are those who won't trust it on that basis alone."

"Including you?" Charlotte asked.

"Oh, yes, absolutely," he answered. "I give anything related to China a very careful second look."

He was still looking intently at her, and Charlotte nearly quizzed him on this point, sensing that he was trying to tell her something without actually telling her. And then Brenda shattered whatever tension there was in the air by reappearing on the runway, all fresh and smiling and "little girl on an adventure" eager for the experience in a small plane.

The flight from Arcadia to Miami was uneventful. Ed had handed Charlotte a map of Florida as the three of them stood by the plane and told her she'd be navigator.

"Navigator? With a road map? Are we driving the plane to Miami?"

"No. Small planes like ours use major features on the ground as markers whenever the visibility permits—mostly major roads. And following a major road has some other benefits too."

He didn't say what these were, and Charlotte didn't have a chance to ask. He was already talking again. "You'll be holding the map, and I'll ask you to hold it up occasionally and maybe help me spot landmarks. It will be too noisy up there for us to talk without help. You and I will be able to converse with headsets. I'm afraid Brenda will just have to enjoy the ride with a noise-suppression headset on. It's not linked into our communications up here."

"Oh, don't mind me," Brenda said. "I'll enjoy the sightseeing."

"We'll go southeast from Arcadia and pick up Highway 27 and follow that all the way down into Miami. You might want to sit on the left side of the aircraft, Brenda. You'll get a good view of Lake Okeechobee on that side. We'll come back along Highway 75—Alligator Alley—across the Everglades and turn north with it and straight up over Fort Myers and back into Arcadia. We should be home before dark, depending on how long your interview goes at Homestead."

Once up in the air, Charlotte found that Ed had been good to his word on how noisy it was. She could barely even hear him when they were conversing with the headsets, and she couldn't hear what she herself was saying in response. Still, she and Ed were in some semblance of contact, and he was dispensing information about what they were flying over that she knew Brenda couldn't hear. The feeling of chagrin returned that Brenda seemingly—through no conscious effort of Charlotte's—was being set aside in the interactions between Ed and her.

This gave Charlotte a slight twinge. But what she remembered most from that flight was how much enjoyment Ed obviously was getting out of piloting and how much he was one with the elements of sky and machine while they floated their way across the Florida Peninsula and down into the congestion that was Miami. He even seemed to revel in the challenge of a close-formation dance with other planes circling and jockeying for position and control tower attention so they could swoop down and land at the Kendall-Tamiami Executive Airport, which was over thirteen miles southwest of downtown Miami. Kendall was a reliever airport for Miami International and a favorite hub for commercial carriers and company jets and small planes.

"This is the airport the crashed plane flew out of, isn't it?" Charlotte asked Ed as he came out of the operations building. Brenda was a few hundred feet off on the grassy patch next to the passenger terminal. She'd been recognized by movie fans—which was frequently the case whenever she went out in public—and she was busy being gracious to them, signing autographs, and posing with them for photographs. Charlotte was amazed at how well Brenda always handled these occasions, especially having come to know just how private a person the actress preferred to be. Charlotte had asked Brenda once about her shyness and being a movie star, and Brenda had answered, "Look at a movie theater, Charlotte. The actors are up there, alone, on a screen. The audience is sitting below in crowded rows. I've never been comfortable in the audience. I can rarely force myself even to go to the premiers of my own movies."

Charlotte was grateful that retired FBI agents generally weren't recognized—or even if they were, they weren't particularly lionized by the public. She wouldn't have gone into law enforcement if seeing someone else in the limelight made her feel a pang of jealously. She was happy to share Brenda's preference for privacy—privacy with Brenda.

"Yes, this is the airport. And the movie company's Miami office must be in a continuous dither about it. The flight plan coordinator I just talked to said they've been calling twice a day to check on any other plane movements by the company. They called today too—both in Arcadia and here, so I guess the office here knows we're in the Miami area. The flight coordinator was surprised we arranged for our own rental car. He said the only reason he could figure out that the office called so often was that they planned to send a car if a plane came in. I guess, though, that they are just very antsy, having already lost one plane."

"And, ah, I see," he continued, "that Brenda has finished with the film fans, so, if you'll accompany me around to the front of the terminal, I'm hoping that our chariot awaits."

"That was a lovely plane ride," Brenda said as they were driving the fifteen miles down Route 997 to the west of Miami's sprawl down the east coast of southern Florida. "I'd had no idea that lake Okee-whatever was that big. I recall that it was the backdrop—well, there and the Everglades—for a Gary Cooper film in the 50s, *Distant Drums*. I had such a crush on Gary Cooper. Little did I know when I saw a second release of that film when I was a girl that I'd be filming nearby too."

Brenda indeed was being effervescent about the excursion in the sky, and Charlotte lost all doubts about having brought her along and then having left her isolated in the back of the cramped plane cabin.

"What, ho. What's that? That's a lot of vehicular barrier array for permanent security."

They were rolling up to the entrance to the Homestead Correctional Institution, a Florida women's prison ranging from minimum to close-hold security. It was where Rose Phan had been held for the dozen years since the facility was converted from a men's prison. Charlotte had been told she was in the minimum-security wing now, considering how long she'd been held with good behavior and how old she was. Although once considered part of a dangerous Chinese Communist spy ring, if not a fully witting member of the ring—either she didn't know everything they were up to or she was a superb actress in her declarations of what she didn't know—so much time had now gone by that no one considered her a threat to anyone else, let alone national security.

It was Ed who remarked on the high level of temporary-looking security at the gate into the facility, which was identified merely by a white-painted concrete headstone-like sign at the side of the entrance announcing that it was the correctional institution. Charlotte had seen it at the same time Ed had, however, the two of them being in the front seat of the car, with Brenda in back, in the same configuration they followed in the airplane. Charlotte's lips pursed as her eyes ran over the black SUVs angled at the side of the entrance road, grills pointed toward the highway, the orange cones necessitating a weaving approach to the gate, and the group of brown-uniformed men, standing around with serious looks on their faces and automatic rifles pointed skyward but available for a downward swivel at an instant's notice.

Ed rolled down his window as one of the sentries approached.

"Sorry, sir, all visitation has been canceled today," the man said, his head dipped so that he could do a scan of the interior of the vehicle. Charlotte noticed his eyes dilate and the little gasp he gave when he saw Brenda sitting in the backseat. Brenda still had that effect on all men, Charlotte thought, with a zing of pride. It didn't matter if the man recognized her as a movie star or not. She has that effect on me each and every time I look at her too, Charlotte added to her thought.

"This is official, I think," Ed answered, not completely sure of himself. "Ms. Diamond here is with the FBI. She's here to interview a prisoner, not visit her. Perhaps—"

"Diamond, did you say? An FBI agent? We were expecting a—"

"A man, you were going to say?" Charlotte said, as she leaned across the seat and held out her credentials for the sentry to see. "A frequent assumption, but not always true. I had been told that the director of the FBI had sent clearances down for—"

"Yes, ma'am, you are expected," the sentry responded, his voice packed with respect now. "If I could just have those credentials and driver's licenses for your companions."

These were taken by the sentry, and he disappeared beyond the gate. He soon was back with a more senior-looking official.

"I'm sorry for the holdup," the official said when he got to the car, this time coming around to the passenger side and addressing Charlotte directly. "But I'm afraid there's been an incident. And you won't be able to interview the prisoner you've come to see today."

"Oh?" Charlottes said, using her "official" voice, which had held her in good stead in the face of bureaucratic red tape for years. "We've flown across the state and I was assured—"

99

"Oh, there's nothing wrong with your authorization, ma'am. I didn't mean to imply that. You can't interview the prisoner because that prisoner's dead. She was murdered in the garden just a few hours ago. You'd best drive on up to the administration building. You'll want to talk to the warden about this. Mind if I hitch a ride up there with you? Then I'll clear you right through to the warden. She'll want to know too why something like this would happen the day you were coming to interview the prisoner."

They were ushered into the office of a very formidable and not-at-all-pleased woman with a statuesque figure and height that rivaled Charlotte's own. And although she gave a close inspection of both Brenda and Ed when the three filed into her office, her gaze rested on Charlotte and she visibly relaxed, immediately recognizing a worthy colleague.

"This is retired Air Force colonel Ed Winslow," Charlotte took the initiative to say. "He's flown us over from Arcadia at the FBI's request. And this is Brenda Brandon. She's in the movies." Charlotte could tell that the warden very well knew that Brenda was in the movies. "The espionage case I was coming to talk to Rose Phan about came out of a movie Ms. Brandon was filming. She's here because she knew Rose Phan years ago and I thought seeing someone she knew would make Mrs. Phan more cooperative." This was a stretch. Brenda had barely met Rose Phan—and that was forty years previously—but Charlotte didn't want her friends shunted out of the office. "And I'm retired—from the Maryland FBI bureau—but the director reactivated me because I'm already down here and working on the movie this all springs from."

"Thank you, Ms. Diamond," the warden responded, slightly less stiffly than the stance she was taking when they came in. "We indeed have received all the documentation we need from FBI Headquarters. Shall we all sit? I believe you have been told that Rose Phan is dead—murdered late this morning. She was in minimum security, so had the run of the prison compound. She was found in the garden, stabbed. It doesn't seem a coincidence that she died on the day you were going to interview her about an espionage case."

"No, I quite agree," Charlotte answered. "Perhaps we should put our heads together. Do you know who did it? Is someone in custody?"

"No one has been apprehended, but a list exists of what guards and other trustee prisoners would have been authorized outside of the buildings this morning."

"And visitors to the prisoners? I understood this was a visitation day. You have the list of who visited who today—and in recent days? I doubt we need go back farther than a week. The case only opened up in the last couple of days, with the crash of a movie company airplane at the edge of the Everglades."

"Of course we have records on the visitors. I did hear of the plane crash. Do you think that has bearing on Mrs. Phan's murder?"

"I'm working on the assumption that it does, yes. A member of her spy ring only recently resurfaced in the States—and was in that plane. And the leader of that spy ring has just been murdered in a prison on the West Coast as well. Whatever is going on, it seems coordinated, wide-ranging, and quite capable."

"Then, yes, let's put our heads together," the warden said.

They did so, and at the other end of the tunnel, Charlotte hit more pay dirt than she had anticipated.

"That license plate goes to a SUV that disappeared from the movie compound over near Arcadia two nights ago. The company's chauffeur, going by the name of Sam Scarloni, disappeared the same night. So, there's our connection. What name did the visitor use?"

"Sam Thompson," the warden answered after she'd consulted the records.

"Tell me about the woman he visited."

"Chloe is one of our quiet ones. I wouldn't trust her an inch, but she's toed the line without deviation, and, if she's been the cause of any trouble, she has been careful not to have been discovered. She runs with a couple of other women, all here for the same crime."

"Minimum security?"

"Yes."

"What were the crimes that brought them here?"

"I'll have to pull their files to ensure I remember correctly. May I have some coffee or tea brought for any of you while we wait?"

Charlotte and the warden had hit it off well, and the warden was quite comfortable and full of hospitality now. Both Brenda and Ed had watched the two professionals work, moving surely toward the intersection points they sought, and they were both quiet, their faces full of awe. All three accepted the offer of something refreshing to drink. The warden and Charlotte had spiraled down to the quick of the issue in half an hour, but it had been a jammed-packed day for Brenda and Ed already.

"Here it is," the warden said. She had quickly scanned the files of four of her prisoners, including the woman named Chloe, who Sam Scarloni—or Thompson, or whoever—had visited the previous day, still using the SUV he had stolen from Carlstrom Field.

102

"They were all arrested in a compound of some rightist vigilantes after a firefight with state troopers. The group set up a regular little kingdom in the woods of Georgia and were robbing from the rich and giving to themselves."

"Does it say in those files what the name of the group was?" Charlotte asked. "Is it the Minuteman Advance, by any chance?"

"Why, yes, that's the name."

"There's your link then. From our fugitive, to your girls here, to, I'll bet, the murder of Rose Phan. Sam Scarloni had ties to the Minuteman Advance. I suggest you start questioning all four of those women. And, if you don't mind, I would like to phone in to my FBI contact."

"Certainly," the warden said, as she rose to arrange for the interviewing of the four women. "And . . . and thank you for your help. The only thing worse than having something like this happen here is prolonging the time before we pin down the who, what, and why."

"The why is still open," Charlotte said. "But I think we're closing in on it."

Then her cell phone connection was going through. "Evan, Charlotte here. I'm down near Miami. We were too late to interview Rose Phan. She was murdered. I think at the instigation of Sam Scarloni. I think that rightist militia group he belonged to, The Minuteman Advance, has something to do with this—but I'm at a loss what."

"You're absolutely right. And I think we know the 'why' now," Evan answered. "I'm already on my way to Florida. I'll be there when you get back to the movie camp. I have just been told we have caught Scarloni. He kept the marked SUV as his ride too long. He isn't saying anything yet, but we know what his connection is, and we should be able to break him down. But just get back to Arcadia. This is too big to discuss over the telephone."

* * * *

"You can be navigator on the flight back," Charlotte told Brenda as they were walking out of the passenger terminal at the private airport in Kendall. She so much didn't want to leave the impression that she had to be the one interacting with Ed all of the time.

"No thanks," Brenda answered. "I'd much prefer to do the full sightseer bit from the backseat . . . unless, of course, you don't want to do it."

"No that will be fine." Charlotte could see from the corner of her eye that Ed thought it was just fine too.

"But I would like to have a map, if you have an extra one up there," Brenda answered.

"Coming right up," Ed responded, with a "glad-to-help" laugh.

They went up into the air gracefully, with Ed again in his element as commander of the flight. He chattered amicably with Charlotte as they turned tail to Miami and headed toward the Everglades high above the straight, eighty-four-mile stretch of Route 75, while Charlotte held the map and strained to hear him in the headset through the noise of the turbulence at this height.

She could tell the instant that he turned serious—and worried—though. He stopped his dialogue on how abandoned pet Burmese pythons were reported to be gobbling up the native small-creature population of the Everglades at an alarming rate in mid-sentence and took on a very serious look. Charlotte could see he now had a white-

104

knuckled grasp of the controls that he had been holding and stroking, almost lovingly, all the way to Miami and part of the way back.

"What is it, Ed?" Charlotte muttered into the headset, instinctively keeping her voice low, not wanting Brenda to hear her, forgetting that Brenda couldn't hear her if she was yodeling at the top of her lungs.

"What?" he asked. He didn't turn to look at her, though, he was peering down from the window on his side of the cockpit.

"I asked if something was wrong," she said in a louder voice.

"Something's wrong with the fuel," he answered.

"The fuel? What—?"

"There isn't any. I checked the tanks before we took off. There should be more than enough to get us there. But now there doesn't seem to be any. Another minute or so and the propeller will stop."

"The propeller will stop? What—?"

"If the propeller stops, we go down. We can glide a bit, but, inevitably we go down."

"What—?"

"What happens is that you see firsthand another good reason why we tend to follow the major roads when we fly. We're going to land down there, on that road."

"Alligator Alley? On that? There's traffic. Is it wide enough?"

"We'll come in with enough notice for the traffic to stop—if they are paying attention. And if you don't pay attention on that road, you go off it and become gator meal. There's a reason it's called Alligator Alley. Hold on tight."

What burned into Charlotte's mind at the mention of "hold on tight" caused her to reach an arm between the front seats to the back

105

and to grasp Brenda' hand in hers. Brenda looked up, giving a radiant smile and waving the open map in her hands, obviously pleased at the contact. Charlotte tried not to look worried as she turned in her seat and looked back at Brenda. There wasn't anyone in the world she wanted to be looking at more than Brenda in these circumstances. At the same time, she didn't want Brenda to catch on to what was happening. Charlotte released Brenda's hand long enough to tug at the straps holding Brenda's body in place to make sure they were secure.

Brenda gave Charlotte a questioning look, and then she began to realize that the plane was losing altitude. And that the propeller had stopped turning on the single engine. Charlotte took her hand again, and the women gripped each other's hands tightly and locked their eyes together, conveying all that each felt for the other, as . . .

. . . Ed Winslow guided the Cessna 172 aircraft into a smooth, gliding landing onto the surface of Route 75. They came in on the tail of three cars whose drivers had heard the plane's approach and who were tearing down the road as fast as they could to stay ahead of the descending aircraft. The oncoming traffic had already stopped, but not without a fender bender or two. Already the drivers of the cars behind the Cessna were honking their horns, as if the Cessna could just rise again and get out of their way.

As Ed taxied along the road, Charlotte found herself, headset and body belts torn off, and impossibly, given the space in the cockpit, in the backseat and tightly hugging Brenda, who was wrapped up like a Christmas present in the shredded roadmap.

There was a shake in Ed's voice—but not nearly the one that he would be justified in having, as he was the first one to speak.

"Sorry about that, ladies."

And then, while both Charlotte and Brenda were declaring their undying love for him for having saved their lives, he spoke again. "First thing I'm gonna do is to take a look see why this happened. You have your cell phone, Charlotte? I figure we're in Collier County. Give your friend, Sheriff Gordon, a ring. He's not gonna love hearing from you, but he'll want to know that we need some traffic cops and a Chinook out here pronto."

"A Chinook?"

"A heavy-lift copter. I suspect that's the only thing that will get this crate off the road now—and if they don't step to it, traffic's going to be backed up to Miami. And those motorists are getting ugly. It won't be long before we may want to take our chances with the gators."

A few people had left their cars and run to the plane to see what help was needed, but most were still in their cars honking their horns and shaking their fists.

Sheriff Gordon indeed wasn't pleased, but he was efficient. Traffic cops on motorcycles showed up in record time—Ed assured the women that this wasn't the first time this had happened on Alligator Alley, or, probably, the last, and that the police had contingencies in place. This highway was one of very few crossing the peninsula, so they had to get it reopened fast.

The cops arranged a cordon of other cops who helped cars slowly move around the downed plane on one side without tipping over into the alligator-infested canal that ran beside it, while Ed tinkered under the plane.

"Just as I thought," he said, as he came up from under the fuselage. "The fuel line has been cut. Just like on the other plane."

"But why didn't the other plane land on the road too?" Charlotte asked.

"Probably because the other pilot wasn't the pilot that Ed is," Brenda said, making no effort to hide the admiration in her voice.

"More likely because it was raining hard that day. The other pilot probably couldn't even see the road to land on. And it was a bigger craft and a jet; jets aren't as maneuverable in an emergency as a good old reliable Cessna 172 is."

"I'm sold," Charlotte declared. "I'll never call a plane like this old and shabby again."

"The plane wasn't far off a highway where he did come down," Ed continued. "Guess I'll need to call back to the Kendall airport and tell them we're all right—they'll know we went down. They won't know we're all right until we tell them. The movie office in Miami will have a fit about this. The Kendall traffic controller said they've been antsy and calling for flight information ever since that other plane went down."

"What Miami office?" Brenda asked. "The movie company doesn't have an office in Miami."

Ed and Charlotte stood there, with their mouths open, processing this information.

"Damn," Charlotte muttered. "Let me make another call."

She dialed and then spoke. "Evan. We'll be a while getting to Carlstrom Field. Our plane went down. Just like the other one, but Ed Winslow is a wonder. He landed on the highway. No, no, we're fine, and no time for that. Tell me, where did you people pick up Sam Scarloni today? Ten miles south of Miami? That's near the Kendall airport— where both planes were. Evan, have your interrogators start asking him what he knows about cutting plane fuel lines. And I can't wait to hear

108

what you have to tell me about this case that you can't tell me over the phone. Yes, yes, we'll get there as soon as we can. Sheriff Gordon of Collier County is here just now and the traffic is beginning to clear. He has a nice new police cruiser. I'm sure he'll be happy to give us a lift—if only to make sure we get out of his county."

Sheriff Billy Ray Gordon was, indeed, exiting his nice new Buick cruiser and walking toward them. Charlotte was happy to see that the expression on his face now was more of an amused one than she could have hoped for.

Chapter Eight: Between Brenda, Evan, and Ed

The chief of the Maryland bureau of the FBI, Evan Worthington, was standing outside the entrance to the main movie camp building at Carlstrom Field when Collier County sheriff Billy Ray Gordon's police cruiser came in for a landing. In fact, nearly everyone in the cast and crew of the movie was on the front drive, talking in low, nervous tones in separate little groups, and all eyes and ears as the police cruiser drew up to the entrance. Tony broke away from the group and was at the rear door of the car, where Brenda was seated, and had the door open and Brenda in his arms almost before the vehicle came to a stop.

Charlotte's eyes were on Worthington as she opened her door and stepped out. She could see the strain evident in the look of concern on his face. As Ed Winslow unfolded himself from the front passenger seat of the cruiser, he too latched onto the concern in Worthington's face—and he had no trouble translating that concern as concern for Charlotte and as having more than just worry for a colleague behind it.

Brenda, with Tony hanging onto her arm, and Charlotte stood with Sheriff Gordon for a moment and expressed their thanks for his help but Ed tugged on Charlotte's sleeve and said, "Brenda and I can finish here. You have company over by the door."

He stood and watched as Charlotte and Evan embraced—the hug from Evan being stronger than Charlotte's—and as the two walked around the side of the building, toward the patio off the buffet room.

They settled down at the table where the doctor had been examining David Runion the previous day. Was it only the previous day? Charlotte thought. Everything before that harrowing experience of the small plane landing on the Alligator Highway seemed like ages ago.

"I was worried stiff about you, Charlotte."

"I was in very good hands, Evan."

"If I'd only talked to you longer on the telephone before you left Miami, maybe we would have given thought to what else Sam Scarloni might have been doing there other than snuffing out Rose Phan so that we couldn't get any more information from her."

"Or if Brenda had been with us at the airport when Ed was telling me someone from the company's Miami office was keeping close check on when someone from the movie company would be in Miami with an airplane—and who that was. Brenda knew there was no such Miami office. I guess Scarloni was intent on cutting off my investigation—by cutting me off. He failed when he found DeeDee in my bed rather than me. So he tried a repeat of the fuel line cut when we flew over to Miami."

"Scarloni was just a pawn in all of this," Evan said. "There was a bigger fish—a much, much bigger fish. That's why I couldn't tell you over the telephone. What we have uncovered up in Washington, based on the connections with the Minuteman Advance that both we and you ran into, is really, really big. And it makes sense out of everything else."

"Can you tell me, or will it be something I will always be wondering about?"

"Oh, yes. Another day or two and it will be all pinned down. Then it will hit the national—and probably the international press—and it will send shockwaves through the political structure of the country."

Evan proceeded to brief Charlotte on the conclusion of the FBI case.

"That's certainly wild," she muttered when he was finished. "And it will undergird just the dynamite movie plotline Howard Holton and Aaron Woolridge were hoping to have for *White Orchid Lost*—if, of course, the government has no objections to us using the themes and the storyline of what really happened."

"None at all, I'm quite sure," Evan answered. "In fact, the current administration will likely be really pleased. It will get one albatross off the president's back. Anderson's commentaries have been whipping the political right up for years and derailing any attempts of nonpartisanship and even the most basic legislation. If he's utterly discredited, the far right might collapse long enough to actually allow some of the nation's business to be conducted."

"Guess tomorrow morning the screenwriting team will be busy—and then the actors and crew can get down to work. They've really been antsy just sitting around here and waiting for something to happen."

"And then you can come back to Maryland, right?" Evan asked. "I've got quite a bit going at the bureau, but I could wait around to tomorrow evening if you'd like to come back with me. I'd like to have

112

you where I can eyeball you—I was scared stiff when I'd heard your plane went down. I thought I'd failed you."

"I don't think you could ever fail me, Evan." Even while saying it, Charlotte was thinking how he'd overthrown her for another woman when they were considerably younger, but she pushed that out of her mind. "But I'm here really for Brenda. And I'll stay on as long as she's needed for the filming. Their plans have been to beef up the part she's now taking, giving the head nurse character she plays and the base commander part David Runion now plays more lines and more a part of the plot, because they are both still box office attractions."

Charlotte couldn't help but wonder if David Runion would be around for this part now, though.

"Ah, yes, Brenda." Evan sighed. "Well, then, I guess I'll start back after dinner—I've been invited to stay for that, and overnight if I want." He paused, but if he was waiting for Charlotte to ask him to stay the night, she didn't do so. "You did great work here, as usual, Charlotte. Won't you come back on board at the Annapolis office as a consultant?"

"I didn't close the case out, Evan. You have. And I'll certainly think about the possibility of future collaboration with the bureau as and if I'm needed. But nothing permanent, I'm sure."

"Why not?"

"If for no other reason than you've twice in the past twenty minutes told me how worried you were for me. That reveals personal feelings that go beyond what's good for the office. You can't feel that personally involved with any of your agents. You know that, Evan. It takes the edge off your capabilities. You . . . we . . . would have to be past our past for it to work. What do you think the chances of that are?"

113

He didn't answer.

"No, I didn't think so. Let's try the friends level for a while and just see how that goes."

He just nodded curtly again, obviously not wanting to commit to anything or say anything that had any finality to it.

"So, I guess we'll see you back in Maryland in a few weeks. You'll have to come down to Hopewell, and Brenda and I'll take you out boating on the Choptank and the bay."

The reappearance of Brenda in the conversation wasn't lost on Evan, and he took it as his cue to retreat.

He stayed for dinner, dining just with Charlotte, Howard, and Aaron. The director and producer were reveling in the promise that their movie would be kick started into action the next morning.

Brenda hadn't appeared for dinner. She'd begged off dining with the rest, saying she was frazzled from the day's events. She said she might come back down after having a nap. Charlotte, however, got the impression that Brenda wanted to give her time alone with Evan. Ed Winslow also didn't appear. He was taking his dinner in his bedroom while, Charlotte was told by Clifford Boyd, the production manager, he packed his bags.

"Packed?" Charlotte asked in surprise.

"Yes, he's left some technical notes, but he said he had pressing business to get home for and that he trusted we now had a storyline that needed more of your expertise than his."

After seeing Evan off, Charlotte remained close to the main foyer so that she wouldn't miss Ed when he came in to check out.

"Were you going to leave without seeing me again, Ed?" Charlotte said when Ed walked into the foyer of the main building with his room key.

"Yes, sorry, I have pressing business—"

"Back in the retirement community?" she asked. "I think we should have a little chat before you go."

"A personal chat or an official inquiry?"

"I'd rather that it not have to be the latter. Perhaps we could talk briefly in the library. They're celebrating the promise of action on the movie so much in the dining room that I don't think anyone will be coming in here looking for a good book to take to bed."

"If we must."

"Yes, I think we must."

When they were settled in the library, Charlotte turned to Ed. "You've known something this whole time. And you've been—not always too subtly—leading me to conclusions. Relevant conclusions, as it turned out. Wouldn't you feel better if you cleared the air? You've come all this way. Don't you think you want to confide in someone?"

"It's all taken care of itself. I don't think . . . well, OK. Do you mind if I tell you a story, though?"

"If that's how you want to get into it."

Chapter Nine: Ed's Story

"The story starts with three young men who are close friends—having grown up together and having lost most of their close relatives. The central young man is the protagonist. One of the others is his older brother, someone he is very close to and emulates. The other is his best friend. It's the late 1960s. The older brother has gone into the Air Force and become an outstanding fighter-bomber pilot, assigned to combat in Vietnam. Of course the protagonist follows his brother, and by the time the decade has changed into the 1970s, they are both flying out of Utapao, Thailand, in F-105 fighter-bombers in the campaign to reduce the defenses, resources, and will to fight in the North Vietnamese capital of Hanoi. The protagonist's best friend, whose eyesight limitations have kept him out of the pilot's seat, has, nonetheless joined the Air Force as well. He is serving with Air Force intelligence in Washington, D.C."

"Can we give our protagonist a name, Ed? It will get tedious, I think to tell your story without names."

Ed contemplated the request for a few moments. "We could call the protagonist Scott, I guess. Just hypothetically, of course."

"Oh, yes, just hypothetically," Charlotte murmured.

But she had a hard time getting that acquiescence out. The name Ed used hit her like a ton of concrete. Why hadn't she thought of this before? Or had she thought of it and just not focused on it? She really was slipping. Her relationship with Evan being too personal wasn't the only reason she was reluctant to consult with the FBI. She'd left service on a professional high. Now she wasn't as sharp as she'd been then. The name 'Scott' brought so much into line. The clues she'd seen and not latched into, even when Ed was trying to lead her to his revelation by the nose. His background; the fact that he had sought this consulting job, had known about the original movie and that it was getting a new treatment. How he had lingered over the crashed Jaguar in the Everglades. Even the subject David Runion had slipped into the previous morning—and how Ed had hung back a bit rather than come to where David could get a good look at him.

"Please, go on . . . Ed," she said. "Do we have names for the other two."

"There's no need for that, sadly," Ed said in a voice that did, indeed, convey sadness. "They aren't on stage very long. But the fact that they aren't is the crux of the whole story."

Ed continued after a pause, during which he'd bowed his head. "In one of the last sorties before he was to rotate back to the United States, Scott's brother—by then a decorated hero—went out on a mission and never came back. The sole pilot who made it back said it was like the North Vietnamese ground and air defenses knew exactly what the mission plan was.

"Within months Scott returned to the States and was assigned to Langley Air Base in southeast Virginia. He was devastated by the death of his brother, and he reached out to the only other best friend he

117

had, who was working Air Force intelligence at the Pentagon in Washington. When Scott described to his friend how well prepared the North Vietnamese air defenses were, which was shocking considering how much of a shoestring operation they were running, the friend became guarded in his responses. But he said there were rumors of leaks—maybe intentional—from high up in the Air Force command. That maybe someone at the generals' level was passing information to the Vietnamese. The friend said that investigations had been launched but had all been choked off at some point in the upper levels of the military. He said that there were some leads he could pursue, however— and that he would do so.

"Scott told him to be very careful. Scott never heard directly from his friend again. Two weeks later, when he tried contacting the friend, Scott was told that the friend had died in a barroom brawl. It was news to Scott that his friend ever drank. He started nosing around himself—as carefully as he could. This led him to Florida."

"To Florida?" Charlotte asked. "Perhaps to here, Carlstrom Field? To a movie set?"

"Precisely. Yes. Scott had considerable expertise with photography. He even was training in photographic intelligence in the wake of his Vietnam War assignment. He had done some work in independent films in college, and he had a few contacts. A wartime film was being filmed in Florida in which he developed an intense personal interest. He pulled some strings, left the Air Force on furlough, and snagged a job as a cameraman on a film here in Florida."

"He was just on a lark, needing a rest from the horrors of war and the death of brother and best friend?" Charlotte asked, goading Ed to drop the pretenses.

118

"No. Not exactly. He was on a mission."

"He was here because a high-ranking Air Force general, Thomas Anderson, was here as an Air Force representative and technical consultant on the *White Orchid* film?"

Ed looked hard at Charlotte. "Do you even need to hear this story? Do you know this story as well as I do?"

"I don't think anyone knows this story as well as you do," Charlotte said. "At least not anyone living. But it was Thomas Anderson's presence that brought Scott to this location, wasn't it? Because Thomas Anderson was that high-ranking general who was passing mission plans and other strategic secrets to the North Vietnamese?"

"Yes. He was passing that information through the Chinese Communists, who were allies of the North Vietnamese."

"As were the Cubans?" Charlotte asked.

Again, Ed gave her a close look. "The Cubans weren't supporting the North Vietnamese as openly, but, yes, they provided whatever aid they could give without being in the spotlight."

"And what exactly did Scott expect to accomplish by coming onto a film set where General Anderson was enjoying a boondoggle outside of Washington and his duties as a Vietnam war strategist?"

"Scott planned to kill the general. As simple as that. A traitor for two loved ones."

"But that didn't happen."

"No. Scott brought a handgun to the movie set for that purpose, but when he got to Florida, two things happened. He fell in love with the young actress playing the role of White Orchid, a love that was reciprocated, and he found out that his love was part of a

119

Communist Chinese spy ring. She was so much in love with Scott that she confessed all. Her brother, John Lu, the screenwriter who had made the film happen, was the spy team leader. The actor playing her brother, Peter Nguyen, was one of the team. And so was an assistant producer, Phan Van Huy, and the company plane pilot, Charlie Teng. All were actually Chinese."

"And they were in Florida to contact the general or to somehow team up with him? It seems a pretty elaborate setup. Wasn't he already in close contact with the Chinese somehow?"

"They were here to fly him out—in the company's small plane, with Charlie Teng at the controls. It was to be a high-level defection at a time when the spirits in the United States and the support for American involvement in Vietnam were at their lowest. It was to be a propaganda master stroke. Something to even top the photos of the actress, Jane Fonda, sitting in the seat of a North Vietnamese antiaircraft gun. One of America's own top strategist generals denouncing the war. He was to be flown out by small plane from this airfield, Carlstrom Field, to Cuba."

"Ah, to Cuba? You almost directly told me this when we were standing over Stephen Taylor's body and discussing the impossibility of interdicting drug plane trafficking into Florida from the Caribbean and South America, didn't you?"

"Yes, pretty much."

"What went wrong with their plan. It never happened, did it?"

"No, it didn't happen. Sondra Tran's love for Scott was the first spanner in the works. When she told Scott what the plan was, he decided that capturing and disgracing Anderson was better than killing him and letting him continue to be lionized as an American hero. Scott had no hard evidence on him that anyone would believe. That's why he had decided to follow the general down here and kill him where he didn't have a lot of protection around him. But Sondra was a foreign spy; she knew things about operations that higher authorities would believe. And she knew where the general fit in. She also would do anything for Scott, so Scott decided to whisk her away from her team and head for Homestead Air Force base, south of Miami, where they would expose the plot and destroy General Anderson."

"Hence the elopement in Howard Holton's Jaguar convertible? But someone tried to prevent it that night?"

"Yes, they tried to prevent it. Scott shot the pilot, Charlie Teng, dead in the struggle—purely in self-defense."

"Which effectively killed the whole spy plot, didn't it?" Charlotte interjected. "No pilot, no defection flight to Cuba."

"Yep. So you can imagine how mad these men were with Scott and Sondra. So, when they drove off in the stolen Jaguar, Phan Van Huy and Peter Nguyen followed in pursuit."

"Peter Nguyen too?"

"Yes. Scott and Sondra thought they eluded their pursuers and made it to a motel south of Naples, where, in the middle of the night, they heard Phan and Nguyen getting out of a car and remarking that Holton's Jaguar was parked in the lot. As the two went into the motel office, Scott and Sondra hurriedly dressed and grabbed their half-packed suitcases. They drove away from the motel and down into the Everglades, with Phan and Nguyen in hot pursuit. Somewhere along the road, one of the spies started shooting at the Jaguar. Sondra took a bullet in the head and was slumped down in the passenger seat of the Jaguar when Scott was hit in the shoulder as well. He veered onto a fire trail leading deeper into the Everglades. But he was losing consciousness and slowing down. The last he remembered for some time was that the Jaguar was being rammed from behind and pushed off the side of the trail and into the swamp."

"And that was the end of Sondra and Scott?" Charlotte wondered if Ed was going to reach for an "out" here. She wouldn't believe him if he did, but it would be interesting to know if he'd try.

He was looking intently at her, and he must have decided that he'd be a fool to try to deceive her now. "The end of Sondra, yes. She was dead before the crash. But not the end of Scott. The two spies obviously thought he was dead, but he wasn't. When he regained consciousness, he dragged himself out of there on foot and back on the main road. He stumbled onto the hut of a swamp hermit, who was happy to believe he was a gangster shot in a local war over bootleg whiskey, a topic dear to the heart of the hermit. The hermit patched Scott up, let him stay until he'd recovered, and drove him back to Naples in a beat-up old truck, not asking any questions, being more interested in weaving his own story for Scott's bullet wound."

"But Scott then just disappeared forever?"

"No, not quite. He stayed around for a while. He no longer had the proof he needed to put the general away, and when he managed to get back to the vicinity of Carlstrom Field, the FBI had arrived and scared the general back to Washington. Peter Nguyen had disappeared too. And John Lu had flown back to Hollywood."

"Only the assistant producer, Phan Van Huy, remained?"

"No, he was gone to. Scott found that he was in Miami, meeting up with his wife."

"And then he mysteriously died too."

"Yes again. He managed to fall from a high-rise hotel balcony."

"While Scott was in Miami, I suppose," Charlotte murmured.

"Yes." Ed said that quietly and gave Charlotte one of his intent stares. He was holding his breath as if his whole life hung on what she'd say next. It was believable that Charlie Teng was killed in an act of self-defense. Not so believable that Phan Van Huy was.

She didn't say anything like he expected, and his exhalation of breath was almost audible in the otherwise silent library.

"But Scott took no further action—toward Peter Nguyen or the general?"

"He intended to. Nguyen had vanished, but the general was back in Washington. Scott went off furlough and returned to the Air Force. He did all he could to be assigned close to General Thomas Anderson, but it never worked out. Scott married. She was a wonderful woman, one who was always looking to the future, not the past. She urged that Scott do the same. She knew he was struggling with something, some unfinished business, but he never told her exactly what that was. She developed multiple sclerosis early in their marriage, and they both coped with it for decades. It's a high-maintenance illness. For all those involved. Scott didn't want to have to leave his wife without the support he could provide, so he chose her over his desire for vengeance for his brother and best friend. And Anderson appeared to go to ground—actually to completely turn around. He became a leading conservative voice in the armed forces. He retired, and, as you know, became an ultraright commentator of great influence."

"And a backer of the Minuteman Advance militant group," Charlotte said.

"Yes. Scott almost let his wife's influence convince him that the man had completely changed. But then it appeared he went too far in the other direction in his change. That's how the FBI connected him with Sam Scarloni, isn't it—through connections with the Minuteman Advance militia?"

"Yes."

"Good. I'm glad he's being exposed at last."

"And Scott came back to help expose him, didn't he?"

"Yes."

"Why now? Anderson has no connection to the current filming."

"First, Scott's wife died. So, the welcome burden of that was off his shoulders. Scott wouldn't be hurting anyone he loved, no matter what he did. And he still wanted to expose Anderson—and still would kill the general with his bare hands if he had the opportunity. But Anderson lives in a virtually armed compound up in Leesburg, Virginia. But there was a way. Scott kept track of those involved in the original movie. There occasionally was talk of trying to refilm that movie. And then Scott saw a feature on how the original director and producer wanted to do a film on the original mystery. And Peter Nguyen's name was mentioned as a technical adviser on the film. Scott hadn't known until now that Nguyen was alive and back in the States and in movies. He was the only one alive and free now—Scott knew John Lu was in custody, and although he'd tried to get to someone in authority in the feds to connect him with Anderson, Scott was turned away as a crackpot. He decided that getting close to the filming of the new movie himself would perhaps enable him to have the storyline cast to expose Anderson and also that, if Scott could get to Nguyen, he might be able to get him to confess to the earlier plot."

"But Nguyen was killed. And John Lu, in prison, as well, and even Rose Phan, Huy's wife, was murdered before we could get to them," Charlotte interjected.

"Yes. Scott wasn't able to complete his mission. Everywhere he turned, Anderson's henchmen were there before him."

"Oh, I think Scott has done very well," Charlotte said. "We meet on the storyline tomorrow morning, and I think that General Anderson will become the centerpiece of the theme of solving the mystery of the original White Orchid film. I would think you'd want to stay around to make sure that . . . Scott's version of the storyline prevails."

"Do you think there's any danger that it won't prevail?"

"No. The planned General Anderson defection is a great story, and I've gotten unofficial clearance to let it rip. They have already picked General Anderson up I believe. There's considerable evidence. It's in the administration's interest to let this all come out—so I don't think there will be any official interference. And I know that Ted Jameson and the director and producer will be delighted with this plotline."

"Good. Then I really see no reason for me to stay around. There might still be some embarrassing questions from those connected with the original film—and from the authorities. I'll leave—that is if you'll let me leave."

"I don't see why not."

"Phan Van Huy. His death. Even Charlie Teng."

"I'm retired, Ed. If no one asks me any direct questions, I'm under no obligation to volunteer any speculation. It's been four decades. I have absolutely no doubt about Phan Van Huy's and Charlie Teng's roles back then. I imagine that Scott will be a central character in both the 1972 and present-day segments of the new film. But of course the film will all be fiction. I'll be happy to leave it that way, if you are."

"Thank you, Charlotte. The best part of all of this was my meeting you. I have thoroughly enjoyed being with you this last week, and—"

"I think it best if we didn't meet again, Ed. It would be the easiest way for us to forget about the story you have told me—the story of Scott. Don't you agree?"

It was a reluctant "yes" she got in response.

* * * *

After seeing Ed Winslow off at the entrance of the main building, Charlotte started to return to the women's building. She couldn't wait to be with Brenda again, and Brenda had retired to their suite before dinner.

Her movement was arrested, though, by hearing a familiar voice singing a sultry song in the lounge, accompanied by a pianist. Charlotte walked into the lounge and sat in a sofa near the back. Brenda was singing torch songs from World War II, and the sentiment she was putting in them—in addition to the sweet, clear tones—almost brought Charlotte to tears.

This was her mate, her love. And Charlotte was overwhelmed that such a beauty—beautiful in every way—could have any interest in her.

At the end of her next song, Brenda nodded to the applause, declared that those were the only songs she had in her that evening, and moved back to stand in front of Charlotte at the sofa. Charlotte raised her hand and took Brenda's hand in hers and motioned Brenda to sit down beside her.

"I thought you were off somewhere with Evan Worthington or Ed Winslow," Brenda said. "I got lonely upstairs and decided to come down for a bit. It's one of those bittersweet evenings, and I just drifted into singing those wartime songs. I'm afraid I don't know any sentimental Vietnam War songs."

"I'm not sure there are any such songs—or much else about the Vietnam War that's sentimental," Charlotte said. "And yes, I was with both Evan and Ed earlier this evening. I was saying my good-byes to both. They're both gone. Back home where they belong."

"And you're sad at the parting?"

"Not particularly. I've done my duty to mankind and the world for tonight. Now, I'd just like to go to bed with my honey."

"I think that can be arranged," Brenda said, giving Charlotte one of her trademark brilliant smiles followed by tinkling laughter. "Shall we?"

Chapter Ten: Lights, Camera, Action

"What are you suggesting by way of a major rethink?" Ted Jameson asked. He was facing Charlotte across a conference table the next morning. They were flanked by the director, Howard Holton, and the producer, Aaron Woolridge. The morning had been set aside for the concept meeting on the script for *White Orchid Lost*. This afternoon the storyline would be presented to the actors and crew, and, they hoped, they could start filming by the next day.

"You've got the mystery of the original *White Orchid* solved now—and I suggest you might want to change the movie title to *White Orchid Found*. And now we have the Air Force general consultant as a natural main villain. In the screenplay concept he was to remain a war hero. So adjustments have to be made anyway. And we have the White Orchid, the screenwriter, the character of White Orchid's brother, the pilot of the company plane, and an assistant producer in the original movie as a Communist Chinese spy ring, with the whole film set up to provide cover for whisking the Air Force general out of the country and to Cuba."

"Yes, that's a strong storyline," Ted said, "And I think changing the title is a brilliant suggestion. But about your suggestion of turning the concept upside down . . ."

"Currently, you are planning to beef up the rolls of the actors playing the head nurse and the base commander for the repeat film," Charlotte answered. "And you didn't really have anything formed for the mystery of the higher-level film about that repeat filming. I suggest you leave the two senior roles subordinate—it's questionable whether David can take his role anyway, and I know Brenda wouldn't mind. This would be interesting because theatergoers will be duped into looking for them to be a bigger part of the plot resolution. And I suggest that you make Scott Carr—the cameraman in the original film who drove off with Sondra Tran in Howard's Jaguar—as the central character."

"I don't understand." This was said by Ted again, although Aaron was looking a bit glassy-eyed too. Howard didn't, though. Charlotte had taken him aside for a private breakfast, and she'd already gotten his backing for the concept she was spinning.

"There was a key element that I didn't focus on well enough at the time," Charlotte answered. "I could kick myself. What was the most noticeable thing about the wreckage of your Jaguar when we first saw it the other day, Howard?"

"The dent in the trunk?" He was smiling and gave Charlotte a wink. He already knew the answer, because Charlotte had already discussed it with him.

She gave a little laugh. She had been throwing a bone to him so that he could impress his colleagues, but he was letting her have the honors. "No, not the dent, Howard. It was what was in the car—and, more important, what wasn't in the car. One body was in the car, in the passenger seat. Just that of Sondra. Where was the other one. Scott Carr?"

"I don't know," Howard answered, playing it for all it was worth. "Maybe he stumbled out of the car and into the marsh and sank."

"The car doors were shut, Howard. A stumbling man isn't likely to think about closing the car door behind him when he staggers off. But it doesn't really matter. His body wasn't in the car. That gives us the opportunity to do whatever we want with his body."

"Whatever we want?" Ted still wasn't getting it.

"Yes. We can even make him alive—and still living—if we want. He can be one of the bridges from the old movie to the new. Peter Nguyen is a natural bridge. He was part of the original conspiracy and he disappeared. And then he came back and was signed on for the movie recast. More than that he was instrumental in rejuvenating the movie concept."

"What was his motivation for that?" Ted asked. "Not just for the purposes of the movie. Why are we here, if that was all Peter Nguyen's plan?"

"That's not really important for us to know—neither for the film or in reality," Charlotte responded. "Maybe he wanted to blackmail Thomas Anderson. Who knows? It doesn't really matter, because what matters is how threatened Anderson felt about digging up the past like this. What's really important is what Anderson set in motion to protect himself. Whatever Nguyen's motive, he died early, and, for the movie, we need him to do that to tie in with the Air Force general cleaning up from the original mystery. But if we have Scott Carr walk away from the Jaguar crash, having been told all about the original conspiracy by

Sondra Tran, we can have him come back for the current movie of the remaking of the movie. He can be someone like the production manager. He could come back to make sure that the Air Force general is exposed as he should be—and he could be standing by the FBI agent the whole time and feeding him helpful clues. We'd have a real hero, if one with some baggage of his own, as the film's central figure. Don't audiences eat up such a movie lead?"

They all paused for a few minutes for that concept to sink in. Charlotte knew Holton was sold. He'd jumped on the idea earlier. And she could see that Woolridge was intrigued by the idea. But he was still hedging.

"Hmmm. I don't know. It seems maybe a bit too 'out there.' Not fully believable. What do you think, Howard?"

Charlotte almost couldn't hold her laughter; Howard wasn't much more in control. Charlotte had sold him on the idea by revealing who Scott Carr had returned to become. "What I think is that it's damned brilliant and will make a blockbuster movie," he said. "The audience loves a stretch—and it will be a charge, as Charlotte said, for everyone to be watching for David and Brenda to make their moves in the central spot, but for it never to happen. I can see the trailers helping to enhance that red herring."

"Yes, yes. I think it can work," Ted said, both warming up to the idea and assured that his bosses would buy it. "Let me work on that. So, we'll make the Scott Carr character the avenging angel of sorts. The hero who is only revealed as Scott Carr at the end?"

"Yes," Charlotte answered. And to herself she repeated the "yes." She thought that would be quite just—that the man now calling himself Ed Winslow would get his just reward. And maybe that he could sleep nights now.

"Of course we'll have to think up good reasons why Carr waited forty years to take action," Ted mused, almost to himself, his mind already working on the script.

"I'm sure you'll think of something," Charlotte said. She could have supplied him with the answer to that to, but she decided that he should work some elements out for himself to justify the big salary he was getting.

* * * *

"So, you aren't upset that your role won't be as big as you were led to believe?" Charlotte asked Brenda late that afternoon when they were alone after the cast and crew meeting.

"No, absolutely not. I'm relieved. And I think it will be a brilliant movie. Making Scott Carr the center is sheer genius. That was your idea, wasn't it, Charlotte?"

"Howard and I agreed to it," Charlotte said. She didn't want to take all of the credit, even though, yes, it had been her idea to give them basically the real story of what happened.

"And what do you think Ed Winslow will think of that?" Brenda said softly.

Charlotte's head snapped up. Brenda was smiling at her. "Yes, I eventually recognized that Ed Winslow was Scott Carr," Brenda said in a soft voice. "The first inkling was when David was suddenly talking about Scott, and he saw Ed for the first time on the patio. Remember, I was in the original movie cast too. David had a breakdown when Scott disappeared with Sondra. It was only years later, after I'd given up trying to land David myself that I realized that David had had a crush on Scott. I had naïvely thought it was Sondra David was interested in. She had that effect on most of the men working on the movie."

"Yes. Ed Winslow is Scott Carr," Charlotte acknowledged.

"And I suppose there is some reason why that isn't being revealed—and that Ed had to go away before the filming even started?"

"Yes, there is. But it's to Scott's advantage. You'll just have to trust me that it's best to leave his real identity known by as few as possible."

"And to reward him for helping you solve this mystery—well, several mysteries—you have made him the hero of our little film?"

"Yes. I think he left unsure that it was all truly over and he could sleep at night. I hope this will be a signal to him that he's safe."

"You're a wonderful woman, Charlotte Diamond."

"And yet I'm not convinced that I deserve you, Brenda Boynton."

"You didn't call me by my stage name."

"That's because you aren't the actress to me. You are my love."

"Do you think you'll take Evan Worthington up on his consultancy offer when we get home to Hopewell?"

"I doubt it. I may dabble a bit, but I was slow to call the key clues on this one. If Ed hadn't been there to throw out hints, I don't know if I would even have gotten into the zone. And it almost got us killed—me a couple of times. I think the thought of retirement is growing on me. And you? I know you're doing this just as a favor to Howard and Aaron. But do you hear the siren call of the theater again?"

"Oh, heavens no. I am relieved that my part in this movie has been downgraded. Like you, I might dabble, but you know we've discussed my idea about establishing a movie actor's retirement community in Hopewell. I'll be pleased to work with that. Seeing David's health suddenly deteriorate as it has before my eyes has been a strong signal to me that it's time to retreat. I wouldn't be surprised if David wasn't one of the first residents in my community—if we can get it built fast enough. My original thought was that the community would be for indigent actors, and David is hardly poor—but I see no reason why I can't be selfish and gather those I love around me."

"Speaking of retreat, DeeDee Yance hasn't retreated, even though I can see that Troy is sticking to his guns and not showing much attention to her. She's still here."

"She's gotten her way. She's here and it's too late to do any more casting. Howard has given her the role of the young nurse. Of course the new thrust of the film has pushed the planned storyline roles of the original characters into the background—hers and Tony's as much as those of the head nurse and base commander—so she'll lose as many lines as I do. I'm sure we'll all hear about that from her."

"In the same vein—the difficulty in recasting on such short notice—do you think David will be able to take his role, even with it cut down?"

"He's already back, and looking better and speaking more coherently. And he's looking at Ted Jameson the way he was looking at Jeffery Morris before the plane crash. David's a trouper. He'll deliver whatever lines they give him perfectly and brilliantly sell whatever character he's in even if he has to come out of therapy and go back into therapy afterward to get it done. It's the law of the theater of his and my generation. The show must go on."

"And from this we go back to digging up our neighborhood to build your retirement community," Charlotte said with a sigh. "I guess I can't get into trouble with that."

"Oh, I'm sure trouble will find you," Brenda said with her tinkling laugh. "I'll bet the day we get home, the backhoe will uncover a pirate's treasure chest, with the skeleton of some Salem witch draped over it, and you'll be off and running again with your sleuthing."

"Oh, please. Don't wish for anything like that. For now, I'm in the mood for a nap before dinner, and I hate to nap alone."

"I'm feeling a bit sleepy now myself," Brenda responded.

"I hope not too sleepy," Charlotte countered.

Brenda's tinkling laugh could be heard across the encampment as the two women retired, arm in arm, to their private suite in the women's building.

DeeDee Yance had retreated to the more comfortable—and prestigious—bed in Charlotte's former suite the moment she'd learned her attacker was in police custody.

About the Author
Olivia Stowe:

Olivia Stowe is a published author under different names and in other dimensions of fiction and nonfiction and lives quietly in a university town with an indulgent spouse.

Books by Olivia Stowe

Charlotte Diamond Mystery Series

By The Howling

Retired With Prejudice

Coast to Coast

An Inconvenient Death

What's The Point?

The Savannah Series

Chatham Square

Savannah Time

Inspirational Christmas collections

Spirit of Christmas (2010)

Christmas Seconds (2011)

Other

Fiddler's Rest